THE NEAR

L. A. JONES

THE NEAR

In the year 2130, the NEAR is the
last place people want to be.

L. A. JONES

Sarasota, FL

PUBLISHER'S NOTE:
This is a work of fiction. Names, characters, places, and incidents either are the product of the author's imagination or are used fictitiously, and any resemblance to actual persons, living or dead, events, or locales is entirely coincidental.

Products and business establishments mentioned in the story are owned by their respective copyright and trademark holders.

For information, address the publisher:
Shore Road Publishing
C/O Concierge Marketing
13518 L Street
Omaha, NE 68137
402-884-5995
ShoreRoad@ConciergeMarketing.com

Paperback ISBN: 978-1-936840-45-8
Kindle ISBN: 978-1-936840-46-5
EPUB: 978-1-936840-47-2

Library of Congress Cataloging Number: 2014920569

Design and production: Concierge Marketing Book Publishing Services

Printed in the United States of America

10 9 8 7 6 5 4 3 2 1

To my father:

He always had that State of Grace.
He shone.
Like light through glass that starts a fire,
He burned.
He ran the race, he fought the fight.
He's gone.
His friends don't seem to understand. They say,
"We thought he'd out-live all of us."
He did.

1

The surrounding neighborhoods ground to a halt in a semicircle a full mile from it, and the ocean wrinkled up against the shore on the eastern boundary. The vast curve of the NEAR eclipsed the skyline as I approached. I had cruised by easily a hundred times during my seven years with the precinct, and cruised a little faster when I did. I could remember reacting on occasion to the flocks of countless seagulls wheeling over it on twenty-four-hour watch, flying level with my squadcraft.

That day, not even my vehicle skimming the edge of their group could scatter the hungry birds. They trailed the massive bulldozers grading the top, their formations lace banners flowing and snapping in the wind. There was something eerily beautiful about streaming by a cloud of white wings. It seemed as if I were being escorted to heaven—except for the smell.

I dropped into a spot near the main building at the south end of the complex. Two figures stood at the entrance, both male, heavyset, sporting screaming-yellow breathersuits with the helmets tipped back, and breather packs. I walked to them. They did not advance to meet me.

"You the detective?" one asked.

The question was common. They probably weren't expecting a detective in his mid twenties, dressed like any civilian, but I had landed in a squadcraft and my badge was visible, clipped to my belt. In most of the city, detectives arrived in unmarked craft. Our precinct was the only one where all officers, even the Chief, rode in squadcraft, except for the undercover teams. The Chief felt it symbolized a "united effort," with every officer having an equal interest in the public's safety.

Still, people wanted to know what they were getting for their tax dollars, so they usually asked, and I usually answered.

"Yes, I'm Detective Edo."

They still didn't step forward to shake hands, and neither did I. The public sets the tone in most encounters. These men staked a perimeter much like the NEAR itself. They said nothing so I filled in the silence.

"I normally have my partner with me, but she was called to another case. Dispatch mentioned you've found an unusual body here."

Their sidelong glances collided with each other. I knew the look: they had either agreed upon one version of the event before I arrived, or someone would pull rank.

The slightly taller, heavier man was doing the talking.

"I'm Tom Reeves, the Operations Director. Bill Corzo here is the on-site boss. His miners called it in. We haven't even gone out to the face yet, just waiting for you." Reeves wanted me to know what I was costing them. Holding up an operation of this size was not popular with these two or the rest of the crew. There was no point in rising to the bait.

"Let's see what you have."

They turned as one and moved toward a massive vehicle the same color as their suits. The second one, Corzo, spoke over his shoulder, "We have a suit for you in the Masher. You'll want to put that on before we get to the face. The Masher has an airlock, like a sub, so you don't have to wear a suit just yet, but first-timers and infrequent visitors seem to want to get one on right away."

I followed, looking forward to donning anything that might combat the foul scent growing on the breeze.

The NEAR, the NorthEast Acquisition and Recovery Landfill, spawned both awe and revulsion. Seven miles long and four hundred feet high, it held the leavings, cast-offs, and garbage from the whole eastern seaboard for the last one hundred fifty years or so.

The NEAR often made the news. I knew more about it than I wanted to: my parents shared a horrified fascination for the place, not unlike spectators who can't turn away from a grisly accident. They hung on every report of a "find," bizarre or precious or both, that no one had seen for half a century, but the profit stream for the fill was the new use for very old paper and plastic waste, chemically combined into Plastrik.

The new substance had replaced concrete block and brick for building. Plastrik wed the lightweight insulation properties of paper to the waterproof virtues of plastic. It also made a great powdered base for 3D printer applications. The best raw materials hid in landfills. Such reuse was amazing.

The stench was amazing, too. The suit helped immediately, so much so that I could almost look forward to reaching the intake tunnel. Almost. I felt the familiar tightening in my chest at the prospect of entering an enclosed space, but I beat it down. I took a last look at the incessant gulls high over the entrance as we dipped into the dark and wished I were in among those wings instead.

The Masher was well named. We slowly crushed odd piles of so-called Stack Trash under the treads on the way to the worksite. On all sides, tunnels ran off into the distance, lit by chemlights in a blue-white haze. Reeves and Corzo pointedly ignored me, the way you resent a piece of equipment you're stuck delivering on your own time, so I was left to educate myself.

I glanced out the nearest porthole at the compacted wall. We passed a doll head missing both eyes, hanging by its tangled hair from a metal shard. A bright green ribbon threaded through the maze of debris for a full ten yards—a shooting star in a smashed universe.

Other detectives who had been to the NEAR said the air was barely breathable, but tasted toxic, because exposure to oxygen after decades of near-vacuum conditions jumpstarted the decay process in the fill and released methane. Although siphoned off and sold, the methane could be present in small amounts, so you stayed inside your suit.

Most mining was done by robots, very sophisticated robots that could tell the difference between Stack Trash and the valuables. The robots had signaled a halt to mining that day. The human workers reacted next, and they called us.

We reached the dig face. It was about fifty-feet high, a mile into the fill. From the airlock, we stepped down onto the flat work area, which stretched out behind us and overhead to accommodate the large shovels and diggerbots and smaller specialized gleanerbots. The many machines should have been humming, churning, crushing, and slicing the walls, crushing and slicing the past.

Instead, they stood at haphazard attention, those with robotic minds puzzled until they powered off their minds and were at the mercy of a human switch to think again. I was sure silence was rare to the point of never in that place.

The chemlights reflected dully from some surface coating spread over a portion of the face. Before I could ask through my headset, a soft click alerted me as someone accessed my comunit, and Corzo spoke.

"Silicone. If we don't put the film up in seconds, the decay starts to destroy anything soft in a matter of minutes, like it's being eaten."

Eating was the last thing on my mind. Even without the smell, the scene before me would have made most people faint or head for the exits. Corzo turned away in a hurry.

In the unrecognizable crush of debris, the robots had marked part of a once-living thing with a circle of gold lights. A left arm with three fingers on the hand created a slight swell under the film about twelve feet above the ground. The arm curved gracefully at the wrist in a still feminine gesture. The ring finger was missing. The sheared-off arm had caught on something where it had dropped onto the dig face from the shovel, but the lights focused on a point in front of the hulking machine blocking my view.

I moved left and forward past a knot of workers staring at the wall. They huddled like worshipers.

In the center of the dig face, like a stage set, a hollow blue LastSteel half dome rested at ground level. The owner of the arm lay on what looked like a tapestry or Oriental rug in the center of the dome floor. The dome created an open space around her about ten feet long and seven feet high at its highest point. The massive sliceshovel had carved into it and through her shoulder before the hoverbots perceived what was being protected. The sliceshovel cradled the other half of the dome in its maw, but for the moment I couldn't think about that. I could only look at the girl.

Aside from the clean cut at the shoulder, her body had kept its integrity. The wound had not bled. She seemed made of something other than flesh, human kindling doused in a congealed pool of silicone. Time and gravity had worked on her lightly, even though the dome was certainly old, and probably ten decades of society's unwanted everything entombed her. That would mean that someone had buried her around 2030. Not a good year—for her.

I had to tear my eyes away for a moment to take in the rest. I knew I had to lay the scene in my mind and take notes. Still, I didn't start my report. I looked at her and gave her my full attention. She asked it. She had paid dearly for it.

The clear silicone replaced the airtight seal that had preserved her, so she had traded one protector for another. LastSteel domes were designed as comfortable decompression chambers in the previous millennium.

They were vacuum-tight and were still being built and used. I knew about them because I had had to decompress in one many times when I had been a repair diver on oil rigs in the Gulf of Mexico, just before I granted myself a different death wish and became a cop.

I walked to within a foot of the film that covered the girl and got down on one knee at her side. Mercifully, her eyes were closed. Eyes do not fare well when preserved by any method, and look like gray raisins at best, tar pools at worst. In the past, coins covered that truth. Shining blond hair fanned out over the rug under her head.

Her skin had tightened almost gently over her bones, as if not wanting to wake her. A white cloth partially covered her. Her remaining arm rested on top of the fabric, and had kept the sliceshovel from cutting the cloth away entirely. Under the cloth she was nude.

The dead have no shame, but she needed none. She had been exquisite, but you have to leave life early to end as a beauty. Her fingernails retained their polish, a pearled wash of color. The uncovered skin bore no scars or blemishes or wounds I could see. There was no way to know what had caused the girl's death, except murder.

The Chief hates it when I know whether someone has died or has been killed. This was a clear case: this girl had been murdered, moved and carefully displayed. She had not died here and had certainly not lived here. But I have never been wrong, no matter how things might first appear. I should wait for reports, findings, and tests. I just know.

When some of my friends have had a few drinks, they've asked me about this "gift," and I have to be drunk to talk about it. I'd like the skill to guess lottery numbers, but instead I can divide death into its two personalities: passive or aggressive.

Death is flushed unwillingly, unexpectedly, from its hiding place in the glare of life by an accident, an illness, a crash. In its other mood, it gets someone to unleash it with deliberation. Who had helped death overtake and devour a girl about to bloom?

■ ■ ■

A detective's job calls for reverse-engineering. The crime is the finished product. You start taking parts away from the mechanism. Some are just there as housing or for decoration, like the smooth skin of a vehicle. As you remove components, the device slows and loses capabilities until you find the piece that stops everything altogether. Here is the moment the crime comes to life, and you find the maker.

My partner and I could reduce this murder to its last/first action, if only to grant the ancient girl a kinder ending. I called in the Collection Agency to gather the evidence and transport the body.

Backup arrived in the form of CyBots. It was odd to have one group of robots, ours, moving all over the site gathering data, like gnats on fruit, while the diggers stood frozen in the exact positions where they were signaled to halt. Some still had their arms extended to within an inch of the face. The hoverbots that stopped the sliceshovel waited in midair for a command like metal marionettes on invisible strings.

In some ways, robots excel at a crime scene. They don't leave fingerprints, cry over the body, or move it. People do. Robots also don't know why someone would kill. People do.

Robots are stupendous at the where, when, how, and who of a crime scene, and do some of that legwork for us. No amount of artificial intelligence can help them with the why.

If their programming captures that fleeting look of animal passion or rage in a suspect's eyes, they calculate the logic behind the emotion and come up empty. It takes a human capable of killing, who doesn't kill, to understand a human who does. A few of us have ridden a motive to the edge, so we know how others might keep going and fall off into murder. Some enjoy the ride again and again. Logic fails.

Our forensic CyBots continued their routine, and I informed Reeves that the site would remain a crime scene. He didn't take it well. I suspended work in the immediate area. I knew it wouldn't last—calls would be made to my precinct. Mining would resume quickly. Stopping even one of the dig sites at the fill burned through revenue, and revenue fights back with many fists.

2

The equipment available to us made it easier to gather the evidence. The sliceshovel carved out the remaining dome section and about twenty feet of the surrounding fill. The news would probably pick up some info, but since the body was so old, it would be a curiosity, not a headline story that would invite much interest. The dome section with the girl would be examined, intact, at a large facility used just for massive crime scene investigations like the reassembly of downed hovercraft.

I thought about the victim. I couldn't help it. She had been someone's child. Some mother had mourned her, perhaps looked for her for years, hoping first to find her alive, and finally hoping just for proof of loss.

That train of thought carried me unwillingly on a limbo journey, to Jack. Jonathan Sinclair Edo, nicknamed Jack, older brother and king of my youth, had gone missing seven years earlier. He was dead, murdered, my "gift" whispered to me. I always told my parents I was still looking, but I had only shifted my focus from finding Jack to finding his killer.

I remembered how my mother and father suffered after Jack's disappearance. I'd had my own ritual. I couldn't close my eyes for hours after lying down to sleep. I would go over everything exactly as it happened the last time I had talked to him. Actually, I had it all on a projection vieunit. I play it sometimes. More than sometimes—so often that as soon as Jack's face takes shape in the air, I'm eighteen again, and I'm with my brother.

What had I missed? I had flown in to visit, on leave from the oil rig for a week's rest. Jack came by, and we had dinner at our parents' home. They retired for the evening to leave the two of us alone by the pool.

Jack took a sip of his third Scotch and leaned back in the chaise lounge. I was sitting forward to his left, staring into the lighted water, when he tapped my shoulder and handed me a blank silver card by the edges, splinter thin and the size of my palm. It came to life as I held it, and my brother's face swam into view on the surface. Jack smiled on screen, and I looked up to see his matching face, looking at my face on his device.

"What is it?"

"ImprinTech. The first person who touches the back or front becomes the only person the device recognizes. It sends only multi-bit encrypted messages and only to recognized receivers. Unassailable privacy. We're calling it the Blade for now," he explained.

"Try it, throw it in the water. The pool cleaner will retrieve it. No moving parts, no battery. The heat from your hand is the only life it knows. When you have messages you want to see as holograms, just insert the card in a vieunit. Boom, big as the room if you like, as long as you're in the room, and alone."

"Is this our company's product? Did you and Dad work on this?" I asked.

"We approved it. Dad can describe it with scientific accuracy. I just plan to sell the hell out of it. I like the simple name, too, the Blade. We all need a Blade. I'm tired of saying to clients, 'I know you want to order more of our XYZ bio-mechanical extenders, or whatever it is we sell. ... Should I place the order for one thousand?'"

I laughed.

"I know the client would like the part about 'whatever it is we sell' and buy a thousand, make that two thousand, of whatever you offered. That's your talent, Jack. People want anything you want."

"Look, I've had too many drinks, but I know when you're trying to bait and switch, get me to talk about me. You know what's coming. I'm here as the liaison for our parents. They're worried about you."

I looked at my brother's face on the Blade. I got up and walked the pool perimeter, tempted to toss the device into the water, anything to avoid this.

"No, Jack, substitute the words, 'disappointed in' me."

Jack made a swatting gesture with a Scotch-induced tilt.

"No, they're never disappointed. Puzzled is a better word. Can you blame them? You are invited to apply to every best university in the country, and what do you do? You go off for a vacation by yourself and come back as an employee of AmOil. What about school? What about the family business? What about that girl you were dating? Did that crash and cause you to crash?"

"No, I broke it off with Geena. She was more interested in my pedigree than in me, it just took me a while to see it. I think she went out with Greg Pierpointe the next day. I'm just ... not sure what I want. I can always go to school. I can always come and work with you and Dad. I can't always dive or be near the water. That's something I know I can't do later. I'll have a family, or I won't have the skill anymore, or the strength, or the balls. It takes something that's in me right now to go into three hundred feet of water in the near-dark to fix a damaged line and do it right, even while the nitrogen narcosis is working against me."

"Then there's the decompression. Hell, I hate it. A little space you can't leave for hours. It's warm and close, like being in the stomach of something. Yet I love the process as a whole. I count on only me. Maybe I need that right now. I don't know what I'll want a year from now, but some people never even ask themselves what they want, they just do what everyone thinks they should."

Jack was silent for some seconds, mulling over my words. I checked the Blade and could see him measuring me although I stood facing the darkened garden and the uncertain night.

"Lot of I's in that speech, little brother. So it's a deadend job, you just said so yourself. You could rent a beach house for a year and still go to school. Dad would stake you."

"I don't want to be staked. Did you ever think about that expression? I just like the ocean. I'm not going to apologize for that. I miss it even now. Have you stood in the shallows on a calm day? A net of light strolls across the sand bottom. Only water can move light around that way."

I walked back toward my brother, who never let me escape without trying to get me to buy what he was selling, and sat across from him. Jack voiced off his Blade and I did the same. He reached over and put a hand on my shoulder. His gaze was so serious I braced for the next lecture.

"Kirt, we need to get you a woman."

We laughed so hard we woke our parents. They told us the next day, and wanted the whole story, but we didn't tell them any of it then. We both went back to our lives. Jack must have defended me to our parents because they didn't say a word about my work, and I stubbornly enjoyed every minute at AmOil. Two months later, Jack was gone.

Because that last conversation focused on me, I felt I might have missed what was about to take Jack from us. It started as a little thought, a little doubt, but carrying even the smallest extra weight becomes cumulative over time and warps the carrier.

3

I had come back from the oil rig to help in the search for Jack, but we had so little to do after the initial investigation and publicity. Jack disappeared from the vehicle garage at our family's downtown offices. In a cruel twist, a smear of cleaning fluid clouded the view on the nearest ScanEye, so the abduction went unrecorded.

Whatever vehicle was used had slipped in between the railing and roof on that level of the garage. ScanEye records from other buildings showed only a distant, fast, black blur. Jack's briefkit and Blade landed on the pavement behind his slipcraft, and one of his shoes had rolled under the strut step. No ransom was ever asked, but we hoped for weeks for any contact. Nothing.

On a quiet afternoon two weeks into the torture of waiting, I stopped to lean against a squadcraft next to a detective who had been left behind at the failed outpost once known as my parents' home. Wordlessly, he offered an open container of throat lozenges to me. I declined. He looked into the distance as he popped one into his mouth and then tried to make conversation around it.

"Kid, you have been a rock for your parents."

The word *parents* came out sounding like "parrots." It was lozenge-speak. "Do you want to know what I think happened to your brother?"

It was an offer, disguised as a question. He crunched on the candy and waited. I almost grabbed his shirt front.

"I want to know anything, just don't lie to me. The other officers said Jack was a random victim—wrong place, wrong time. There was nothing suspicious on his I-net or in his briefkit, only appointments. Whoever took him didn't even want his gear. Why Jack? Everyone liked Jack."

"Kid, your brother was by all accounts a great asset to your family's business." He leaned toward me, twitching with conviction. "I think it was corporate espionage. The Bio-Mechanics industry is very lucrative. Big, big money changes hands. There are people who must come out on top. Losing a single account is like having your treasury raided," he said.

"Your brother brought down countless competitors. They were watching him. They waited until one little camera failure gave them an opening. Your security people cooperated fully. No one left suddenly, there were no new hires. Maybe no one was paid to watch for that opportunity, maybe someone was paid, but we lack evidence either way. It was all just too good to be true, so I looked for an angle."

I must have been leaning toward him, waiting for the motive I hadn't considered, not forgiving myself for being eighteen with no experience measuring such a monstrous event. He longed for a fresh listener, as essential to him as his theory.

"Your family's business has suffered since your brother's loss. I watched the stock exchange, and your company's stock fell out of the stratosphere like a fuc---, uh, like a goddamn hovercraft failure, excuse my language."

He went on, "Espionage is the only thing I can see that would make it worthwhile to take a very visible guy and make him invisible. It had to be done by somebody really good, a real pro. Anybody that good has to brag to someone, or at least some street mythology builds around him, but all my informants came up empty, didn't hear a whisper, not even for a reward. Maybe, maybe your brother's a captive and they're getting information from him and will let him go. That's why there's no ransom. They may keep him a while ..."

He let this trail off, and I think it was because he didn't believe it, but just couldn't say that to me. I had wanted the truth. A softness came into his eyes, the same look I had seen around our home when the detectives spoke to my parents, the kindness reserved for those who might have to master the art of open-ended despair.

"I haven't told any of this to your folks. I was overruled. There isn't any evidence to support me, just a feeling. Still, I sometimes think it's better to have an idea why your kid is gone, even if it's the wrong idea."

I thanked him even for bad news. I didn't see him after that day. I thought about telling my parents, but I feared it might have all the wrong results. My father might blame himself for putting Jack in danger. My mother would live in fear for my father and me every time we left the house. I struggled with what the detective told me. No wonder he had asked first if I wanted his theory. That way, what I did with the information wasn't his problem.

I couldn't sleep for nights while I decided what to do. Something about his idea kept bothering me. Jack just sold the things our family's company created. He didn't take the long view. He wasn't interested in the talks about development, just a shiny finished product, like the Blade. Jack, even at twenty-five, was the enthusiastic kid with the new best toy, convincing everyone to get one so they could all have the same fun.

I finally decided to keep the detective's ideas to myself, but those long hours lying awake made me aware of my mother's restlessness. She would walk softly by my door at about three each morning. I could hear her trying to stifle her sobs, but I wouldn't go to her immediately. She needed the solitude, away from my father, and me.

After a while I'd go out to her. She was always curled near the right end of the massive sofa, her head resting on her arm, her golden hair knitted softly to her cheek with dried tears. I would touch her shoulder, which made her look at me through swollen eyes. She'd let me draw her up to walk arm-in-arm to my parents' bedroom door.

My father slept through this, or gave the appearance of it. He suffered more in the daylight, spending hours savagely uprooting and moving plants and small trees in the greenhouse with the sun pouring in on the carnage. Grief does a different dance with every partner. My father destroyed and rebuilt the entire greenhouse before he resigned himself to Jack's loss.

My mother was fairly young then, but seemed to age terribly after we lost Jack. She begged me not to return to AmOil, to oil rig diving, her face a map of agony she couldn't hide. Diving was a dangerous thrill, and she was terrified that if one son could be lost in an ordinary-looking day, why invite daily peril to take the other?

Jack's disappearance made me the older son, in every way. Two things became important to me: finding Jack, or finding those who killed him. There are few avenues to travel when hunting for someone. You hire help, or you do it yourself. I chose to join the police force. I told my parents I wanted the skills to find my brother.

While I had expected fierce resistance from my mother for choosing another dangerous line of work, she seemed to accept it, perhaps because I would be trained to avoid death rather than court it. I got a university degree via the I-net in a single year while graduating from the police academy at the top of my class. Doing both took grueling effort. I hardened into something past grief. It felt good not to feel.

At twenty-three I fast-tracked to detective through an experimental "PUSH" program: Promoted Under Supervision/Homicide. Everyday police work on the streets had been handed over almost completely to the robotic staff. The department discovered they needed fewer enforcers and more solvers.

Still, I was the youngest ever to pass the aptitude tests. It was also in part due to my magnified thirst for police work—and my family's connections. I took all the steps, from beat cop to hover patrol to sergeant to detective, just earlier and faster than others.

I earned a reputation on the firing range too. I was good, very good with my lasermagnum. Squad members found reasons to drop by when I did my mandatory qualifying. The targets exploded and fell into confetti when I blew open the kill zones. The other cops wouldn't have come to target practice if they hadn't seen me kill someone. In fact, resentment from other officers would have destroyed my career if I hadn't been able to prove my worth.

When I was promoted to detective, they paired me with Carl Bryce, one of the oldest members of the squad. He was not happy, initially.

I saved Carl's life during a smash and grab we responded to because we were practically on top of it. As we landed with weapons drawn and gave chase, one of the perpetrators was willing to die if he could take someone with him. He turned and targeted Carl.

I am told I dived across the space separating me from Carl, firing as I shielded my partner, taking out the gunman just before I hit the ground with my shoulder. I don't remember doing it, but others on the scene wouldn't forget it. Photalk versions of it made the news instantly.

Carl didn't forget either. We were sitting in a quiet bar after work about five months later when Carl casually mentioned he was retiring. He was forty-nine. I was shocked, and my voice must have shown it.

"Why? Is it me?"

Carl launched his "clipper ship laugh," as I called it, because it sailed around the room and hoisted everyone aboard. I joined him. I couldn't help it, even if his next word might be yes.

"Hell, no. If it weren't for you, I wouldn't be here to leave." He laughed again. "I wouldn't be here to leave, that's a strange turn of words, isn't it?"

His face changed a little, something I caught that others might miss. He took a sip of his beer to try to hide that shift in his demeanor before he spoke again.

"I got careless, at that robbery. That hasn't happened in about twenty-five years. All it takes is one moment's inattention, one damn, very dead, moment, Kirt. Hey, don't look like that. I'm glad to leave now. Just remember, youth isn't everything. In fact, if my enemy is age, your enemy is youth. I guess that's why they put old guys with young guys. The experience and the youth average out somehow, and we end up trading some of it. But because you're so young, and I'm so experienced, I'll end up being a juvenile delinquent, and you'll end up being ..."

The enormity of his leaving suddenly overcame him. Carl drew his hand across his trembling mouth. He tried again.

"You'll end up being ..."

He looked a little desperate. It seemed up to me to bring this home somehow.

"Hey, Carl, I'll be happy to just end up being."

Carl laughed harder than usual, and it rolled to the walls and back to wash over us both.

He dropped out of sight after his retirement party. Three months later, I got a postcard from Carl, an actual postcard, with an actual casino chip taped to the back, and a message under it.

"Push this button to start Las Vegas."

He called two weeks after that. He had a girlfriend, Linda Red Horse, of the Jicarilla Apache Nation. He later sent a hologram of the two of them, standing before a little house. He looked ten years younger, due to the effect of the light or happiness or both. Linda had that long gaze of her people that took in the landscape and eternity and melted them together.

They had married. She was pregnant in the image he sent. He asked me to come for a visit, and kept asking. I did finally get time off, taking a quick air transport to land in Las Vegas on a blistering day. The buildings actually seemed to bubble in the cooking heat. Carl threw his arms around me at the gate. He drew his wife forward, and she held a round little boy in her arms. His soft hair stood straight up in a static response to the tiny cap his mother lifted off his head. He looked at me with curiosity, and clung to the index finger I offered: pals at once.

Carl and I sat in two chairs on his drivepad and sipped beers. It was dusk, so it was more comfortable to be outdoors. We faced a distant range of low hills. There was no way to tell how distant. The clear air magnified the view. They could have been across the road at the end of the drivepad.

Maybe it was the drinks, but everything eased up, like a rail transport slowing into a station. Carl leaned back and stretched his arms to the sky, then laced his fingers behind his neck and looked up at the stars beginning to appear.

"Man, it is so great to see you, Kirt. Wait until you see the Boulder Dam. Lake Mead has been high and full, so they've opened the sluice gates more than usual. Just the sound of that water set free will make your blood leap up and want to follow it."

"As long as we can sit right here, right now. I like this, very much."

I looked over at him, and he was smiling into space. We talked of his son, Carl Junior, and his dark-eyed, much-loved wife, but he didn't drown me in tales of his new world. We talked a little about me and my string of temporary partners, but I wanted work to stay in the distance, like the hills, and he sensed that. Mostly we enjoyed a companionable silence until the moon rose and Linda called us in to dinner.

After the meal, I brought out gifts I had for each of them. Linda shyly took a small box from my hands. She opened it to find a silver filigree brooch, centered with a fire opal the size of a quail egg. She did not move for a minute, then took it from its velvet bed and pinned it to her blouse. The colors moved across the face of the stone as she came to hug me. For little Carl, I had a tiny toy hover car like my old favorite. He was too young for it, but it was a toy for his future, from my past.

I handed Carl a long flat box worn shiny at the corners with age. Inside, a pearl-handled pistol gleamed as if it had just been pulled from a holster. There was no ammunition, as none had been made for it in countless years. It was a tamed symbol from a wild West we now only read about as children, but there was no denying its lethal beauty even centuries later.

Carl picked up the relic by the handle and rested it across his other palm. He looked at me with a kind of reverence that made me uncomfortable. I wanted to lighten the moment, but it didn't come out that way.

"Carl, it reminded me of you. It did its job, with style. Now it has a new home, actually its old home. It's where it belongs."

He cleared his throat.

"Well, I … what a … hey, we have something for you, too, but it isn't here. You'll have to wait until tomorrow.

Until then, I haven't got the words to thank you, except, thank you. These things are all perfect and special. Hell, I'm lousy at this. Linda, is there any more of that cake?"

We left the house at 10:30 the next morning, all of us, and packed into Carl's small GMX. We had to share the little vehicle with some outdoor gear. Carl took a low flight path toward the range of hills we had viewed the previous night.

We landed about one hundred feet from boulders strewn like a lazy necklace around the throat of the rising landscape. Linda hoisted Carl Junior into the sling across her chest, one smooth motion in the beating sun. I offered to carry him, but she smiled and shook her head. She adjusted her hat and Carl Junior's cap as she spoke.

"We will walk for a while, and you are not used to the heat. You will have enough to do to carry yourself."

Carl shrugged on his backpack full of iced water, shoved a wide-brimmed hat on his head and one on mine, and we set off due west into what looked like a long canyon. It sloped upward, and every step seemed to bring us a degree closer to oven temperatures. Carl handed me a steady supply of water. The three of them appeared unaffected by the climb.

After several side paths and some winding trails, we turned left into a wide chasm, running north and south. Soaring walls held out the slanting light, which was still working its way toward high noon. Carl let Linda take the lead with her mile-eating stride while he walked beside me, talking in a low voice.

"I would have brought you out here when it was cooler, but we had to come now, at this time of day. You'll see why in a minute."

Linda had stopped, and she turned toward the cliff face on our left, still in shadow. We came to stand next to her, and Carl looked at his watch. As the sun hit its zenith, it began to illuminate the cliff face from the top.

Suddenly, what had been mere rock became a huge mural. In the reverse of what was normally done, what was not picture had been carved away, so the image stood out in stark relief. A map of a lost world blazed out at us. Pictographs showed people, and villages, and animals running in a stylized rush to the borders of the carving. Rivers and rocks wove the world together. Linda spoke in a voice that echoed softly off the wall in front of us.

"It is a map of this place, when it all belonged to one tribe, but we don't know their name. It is so accurate that Carl and I found the now-dry river beds and the rock formations nearby. There is no trace of the villages, heat and time ate them up. I think we are the only ones who know this is here. We found it by chance and never told anyone—except you. It is not just made of symbols. The map itself is a symbol, and a warning. They knew they were a great people, but also that all things rise and fall, like the sun."

Exactly as she said it, the light shifted farther west and illuminated the cliff face fully. The mural disappeared into the irregularity of the rock, and was gone.

We stood there, shoulders touching, until Carl Junior shifted in his sling and woke with a hiccup. We laughed and broke the gravity of the moment, in that chasm holding the present and the past.

I stayed four days and saw Boulder Dam and saw that Carl was the happiest man I knew. Just before I stepped aboard the transport, he draped an arm across my shoulders and spoke in a slow, Western drawl, "If you ever need me I'll come right away, but … think three times before you call, or better yet, come get me, and bring your partner and a long pole."

"Pole?"

"You'll have to truss me up and carry me out on it like a bagged stag to get me away from here."

It was a great mental picture. I sailed off on Carl's laugh.

4

When Carl retired, I faced a challenge. None of the other detective pairs needed change, so a string of detectives followed. Bringing in a new personality required building a new routine, but what difference would it really make? I was about to learn the hard way.

I was first paired with another veteran detective from the 7th precinct, Duke White. He showed up the first day without his badge. He left it on his kitchen table, he said. He leaned forward to tell me, and I realized he must have left his badge on the table next to the bottle of Scotch. He called in sick the next day.

He finally appeared on the third day, alert and presentable. The pattern continued: bad day, sick day, good day. I finally pulled him aside on a good day and told him to get treatment or I would have to write him up myself.

He hung his head and admitted he couldn't go on working. His wife had left him. He turned in his badge. I did get him into a program and stopped by his house twice. His hair was combed, and there was food in the refrigerator. We drank iced tea. Three weeks later, he used an unregistered weapon with no ID code to speed himself into the next world. So much for the comfort of tea.

Duke's ex-wife and I were the two mourners at the service. The department stayed away from suicides, but created a Roman spectacle for officers who died in the line of duty. How the end arrived made all the difference, but it still arrived. Someone with unschooled hands still took the urn to its little crypt. Someone still wept, then or later.

My next partner was always on time and never called in sick. I wished he would. Detective Dieter was a freak in the cop world. He loved reports, and he loved the statutes. His write-ups went on for days, it seemed. He could quote the law on anything, to anyone. The Chief even tired of it and told him he had to keep his vid-file documentation to three pages. The tome he created would finish with something like "Page 11 of 3."

Since you can't really fault an officer for liking files and even actual paperwork, the Chief gave Dieter a special title and moved him into the evidence room where he could track things and check materials in and out all day. Dieter was in his element, and I looked forward to my next partner as I would dental work.

I was sitting at my station, pounding out a report on the tiny Speedict screen, when the Cave grew quiet. Our equipment is so archaic, along with a few of our detectives, that we call the squad room the Cave. The Cave is never quiet.

I looked up to find a woman standing in front of my console. You would not look at her first or last in a group of people, but her coloring was striking—a contrast of light and dark, with deep gold eyes. It was her demeanor that caused the dead silence. She had the look of an Olympic decathlete.

Although she was standing still, she wasn't, really. Everything about her said, "Ready." No braid could completely tame that flow of chestnut hair. The dark gray jacket and skirt could not hide a lithe frame, flexible and movable in the wind. That was it. She always appeared to be outdoors, not held captive by anything. A lock of hair fell over her cheek as she tilted her head to one side.

"You are detective Kirtland Edo?"

I felt a little off-balance, as if I were tilting along with her. Now I knew her magic. Once you heard her speak, you would go anywhere just to hear her again. You could eat that voice with a spoon.

I looked into eyes framed by dark lashes and replied, "Yes. I also answer to Kirt."

She put her hand out between us just as I did the same.

"I am Suli Masters, your new partner."

It took a while to build on that first brief exchange. Now, we speak of all things, at all times. Well, almost all things. At work, we are two halves of one mind.

We became legend, not meaning to do that. When we would appear at a crime scene, the paramedics, other police and forensic teams, and robots would part like the Red Sea. We noticed it after a while, so one day at an off-duty hangout, I asked one of the paramedics about that standard reaction. I thought it was the Suli Effect, the Suli Voice, but his answer surprised me.

He said something like we were the proof of life when we showed up at a crime scene, as if we brought certainty of justice. It was a feeling people got when we were around, he said. He looked embarrassed by his own words, and went back to his beer.

Proof of life? Suli deserved her share of their trust. I wasn't as sure about mine.

5

When we had been partners for two weeks, I told Suli I liked her suit. She smiled and told me I had just praised 25% of her total work wardrobe, then immediately rolled her eyes at her own words.

"Kirt, I am so sorry! I shouldn't have said that. You gave me a nice compliment, and I made it into a commentary on my life. You might as well know, though, since you will have to get used to the same four suits for a while. I am putting my funds into home improvements, school loans, that sort of thing. Oooh, more life tales. Stop me any time."

I couldn't tell her it wasn't the suit, but the lean, lovely body that drew my attention—the way her hips moved under that skirt, the sheen across her collarbone just above the first button of her blouse. No, couldn't tell her the real reason.

"Suli, I'm interested. I know almost nothing about you. I used the 'nice suit' thing as an opener. We may be sharing this squadcraft for a long time, and it would be bad to know more about someone in restraints in the back than I know about my own partner."

"Well, well, I … hardly know you, either. You first."

"No, ladies first, or 'Pearls before swine,' as someone named Dorothy Parker once said."

Suli laughed. "You are not a swine, but I am a pearl. Fair enough. I have an idea. They always say show, don't tell. Head 270 degrees and I will let you know when to start descending."

We passed over the rich meat of the city and headed for the leaner parts. We turned to 180 degrees and cruised south over what had once been the Hudson Parkway, until we dipped onto a short side street. Suli told me to slow down and look to my right.

On the third story of a bleak apartment building, planter boxes of red geraniums brightened the sills of four windows. I made every effort to sound upbeat. It was an oasis in a crime desert.

"Your place?"

"No. My parents live there. I grew up there."

She turned to me as I had the squadcraft at hover next to the building. Suli sat tall, proud, and animated.

"I come from nothing except two great parents, from an apartment held together by hope and flowers. I am guessing that, whatever your past is, it isn't like mine."

We lifted away slowly as Suli opened her life to me. "My father managed the apartment building, which allotted him a unit there. That's how he met my mother. She moved in along with her parents, just after she had finished college and hadn't become anyone yet," she told me.

"Her family had moved so often Dad said she was like a self-contained traveling show, needing no one, only giving enough information to outsiders to keep them entertained. When he told me that about her, I didn't believe him. She's always been sweet and warm as new bread to us. He told me he changed her by being everywhere and constant and comfortable, like furniture."

She went on, "It worked. Here I am, proof. Oh, and the flowers, she always plants flowers in the window boxes."

She had been scanning the neighborhood below as she talked. I stopped our slow ascent and hovered in place again until she looked at me.

I said, "That's their story. What about you? Maybe you got your mother's 'entertain the outsiders' gene."

Suli's eyes opened wide. She blinked a few times.

"I … you're right. I never start with me. But maybe it takes one to know one."

We both said a silent "oh," pointed at each other, and grinned.

"Point for Suli Masters," I said, caught in her revelation. "So tell me more. We'll get to me later, I promise."

"Okay. See that fenced playground below us? First kiss, from Danny Barron. I was fifteen. Should I start further back, when I lost my first tooth and thought I would get a new tooth under my pillow rather than money? I didn't think so."

While Suli moved around in her past, touching the highlights for me like a guide in a museum, I realized how rare she was. I had experienced only the criminal poor. Morality is often a luxury that forces the poor to aspire to it or live without it.

Suli had come from the honest poor, had breathed in the same desperation as the criminal poor, but she breathed it out while they inhaled it. She had lived among them, and they could have touched her, but her fierce goodness would have burned their hands. Suli had climbed up through life from that third-story home and reached the academy.

After she fell silent, I told her about Jack, just like that. I started talking as we headed back to the precinct, and I couldn't stop. Instead of the usual wide-eyed, "Oh, I'm so sorry! How terrible!" or some equally automatic response, Suli closed her eyes and laid her hand gently on my sleeve for ten seconds, saying nothing.

It was one of those moments in life when a person does a thing that suits you, not the expected thing, or the known thing, but the perfect thing, without knowing it is for you alone. It was the first hint she fit me as if measured for me. There is a terrible burden in knowing a person can be this for you when you do not know if you can be the same for them. How do you do what can't be learned?

It was a puzzle, the kind you work, then leave for a while so you can come back with a fresh eye. In my world, every case was a puzzle, but she became my most important case, even more important to me than Jack. I just couldn't let Suli know it.

There was one thing Suli asked of me as a fellow detective and partner. Suli wanted me to look along the length of people, to look for dimension rather than just flattening them against the present, in order to see the history that caused them to intersect with me. I tried for her sake. Most suspects didn't make it easy for me, but Suli had no trouble. When one of them sneezed, Suli said, "Bless you."

I saw Suli's way with people the first time we stood over a savaged body in a particularly popular alley for drug dealers. As the Collection Agency sorted through the pieces, we spoke to two men the patrolbots had briefly interviewed and asked to stay. I had seen them both in the area before, many times.

I asked my witness, such as he was, if he knew anything about the deceased. He looked at me with glazed eyes and said he was on his way to get milk when he turned to see movement in the alley. It was a blur, he said, as he looked past me to see the forensic vehicle rise up slowly and drift away toward the morgue. They had no reason to hurry now.

My witness tilted his head and watched until the craft disappeared over the crumbling buildings of the neighborhood. He seemed to have forgotten I was there. I cleared my throat, and he rediscovered me.

"As I was saying, officer, I didn't really see nothin', just a quick blur."

"The victim had multiple stab wounds and was beaten. His hand was nearly carved off at the wrist. That would take some time and effort ..."

I let this hang in the air. His eyes slid off me.

"I just ... didn't really get a good look at anything."

I excused myself for a moment and walked over to Suli, in mid-interview with another onlooker. She asked her witness to please stay and stepped aside with me. I must have looked amused, maybe a little resigned.

"My witness was apparently very interested in getting milk, so interested in fact that he didn't see anything. Even if he had been standing over the killer during the act, he wouldn't have seen anything. He's evasive, but he can't be blamed in this area."

Suli looked directly at me and gave me a measured look.

"Come down from there."

I didn't have any idea what she meant and my face must have shown it.

"Excuse me, what?"

"Climb down off your badge. You get to ride out of here in a while, these people can't. Perhaps he's afraid. Let's go talk to him again."

She strode ahead of me to my witness and put her hand out to him. He paused and shook it. Suli spoke in her silky voice, "I hear you were on your way to get milk. Let's go get it, my treat."

He followed her, as I did, to the tiny market with barred windows, which stood at the corner of the alley. We watched as he stepped in front of us and approached the cooler. He peered through the door with his face almost at the glass. He pulled on the handle and a wash of cold air poured out into the aisle. He looked at the quart containers and chose one with a red cap.

"If they ever change that red cap, my old lady will be mad mad mad. Red cap means whole milk. Only kind she'll drink."

He looked at Suli.

"You don't really have to buy the milk, officer. I got the credits for it."

"My pleasure. We have delayed you for almost an hour. Need any cookies to go with that?"

Suli held a package of something other than cookies in front of him.

"Oh, she don't really like cookies, but thanks all the same."

Suli paid for the milk and we left the store. She told my witness we would contact him if we had any more questions. She shook his hand again, and he disappeared around the corner. Suli smiled slyly, tilted her chin up, cupped her ear with her hand, and waited.

"Okay, Suli, he really actually can't see well. My mistake. My assumption. But hell, this is the third murder within two blocks within six months. I have heard, 'I didn't see anything' so often, I'm beginning to think it's a photalk lesson taught to the neighborhood."

"Don't let 'I didn't see anything' become your own excuse for, well, not seeing things. People reveal themselves when they are comfortable, or off-guard. You have a way of looking like you're arriving with the Ten Commandments. You are so good, Kirt, at figuring out the facts. I am the one who figures out the people. It works, but I want to learn from you, and you could learn from me."

Her voice made anything sound reasonable. Still, I wasn't seduced. Well, a little.

"What's wrong with the Ten Commandments? You have a point, but we don't work very often with the innocent population, Suli. Carl, my previous partner, let his guard down and almost died for it. Some people ask if I even bend in the middle, but I'm alive to hear them ask. I don't relax out here."

"Don't! I know you saved Carl's life. Teach me how to do that. Just try to look a little deeper, that's all."

She had me thinking about it the rest of the day. Damn, she was good.

...

I wanted Suli's input now on this NEAR case, the strange display of the body, and cursed the luck that had sent Suli to a call across town. I had been headed there when I was rerouted to the landfill scene since I was nearest the vicinity.

Missing persons cases always bothered me. Even if there was no one left alive to miss this girl, I wished someone could know that we found her. We did talk about it later, which helped me put it in perspective and pay attention to Suli's case. It was a double murder, actually a homicide-suicide.

To me, suicide is murder. A person turns on himself with means, motive, and opportunity. The only difference is that it makes the killer easier to find. We both had paperwork on what I felt were solved cases—hers because the clear evidence supported the conclusion, mine because any conclusion was too late to matter.

Two days, and our forensics star, Jana Jessup, would change every supposition.

6

Monday morning, Jana came to stand, as she always did, at the center of the front of my station. Always before today, as she talked, she would run her finger slowly along the edge of my console, first left, then right, and follow her finger with her eyes. She never looked directly at me, but would give her account of an autopsy as if she were delivering a soliloquy from Shakespeare. Her pronouncement always started with, "The deceased."

"The deceased," she would tell me, "a man in his thirties, was drowned, but was first struck with a blunt object, almost certainly a baseball bat, on the left rear quadrant of the skull. No other injuries, his mother could be heard keening for blocks around during the ID. Why is life so short for some?"

I understood why Jana spent most of her time with the dead. Her skills with the living needed work.

This time, Jana surprised me. She looked right at me.

"The girl from the landfill."

It varied from "The deceased," and Jana was strangely animated, not dreamy. I had expected a brief report and stopped her.

"I didn't think you would spend much time on her, Jana, since she has to have been around for decades. The perpetrator has to be landfill, so to speak, by now."

"Detective Edo, would you come outside with me for a moment?"

I had never pictured her "outside." She was in forensics, not known to much enjoy the light of day.

"Of course, Jana."

I followed her through the building to the squad lot. Jana looked down and bit her lip before speaking, something my suspects did when they were finally going to confess, the body making a last effort to withhold the truth.

"I wanted only you to hear this."

"I'm listening."

"The girl was about twenty years old, from the bone maturity. Cause of death was by injection of a lethal substance, still getting the report back on that. No other marks, no sign of a struggle, fingernails are clean, no tissue trail there."

"Sounds like other cases. Jana, why are we out here?"

"Her nail polish intrigued me. It matches a sample in our spectrograph, but there is something odd. It contains a synthetic replacement for mica, the original ingredient in this brand of polish."

"And, so?"

"So the new synthetic was recently added. She is wearing polish less than four years old. She has been dead less than four years."

I had expected anything else, but at least something possible. My vocabulary failed me.

"What?"

"My reaction, so I did more tests. Make that many more tests. Her fabric covering is old; everything found with her is old. Her killer added those things. The killer wouldn't go to lots of trouble to find old things to surround her, and then paint her nails with a new polish. She had to have painted them herself. She alone is new, possibly very new, although her state of preservation makes it difficult to determine exactly. That is not all."

Jana put her hand on my arm. "I did a DNA search, since I now knew she was a recent homicide victim. I got a partial match. She shares several DNA markers with you. You are related."

It didn't matter that I didn't know the girl. DNA doesn't lie. I'm not sure what my face revealed to Jana, but I felt dread as if it had started raining dread. I began to think aloud.

"And of course we don't know who she is, because we don't have her DNA print."

"Correct, Detective Edo, we do not."

After seven years in police work you know certain things. DNA printing had become mandatory about thirty-five years earlier. Every child born on the planet was to be printed at birth. It was such a simple procedure now, just a swab of the mouth, or even a lip print if the person had moistened their lips with their tongue.

The profile was available in minutes, filed seconds afterward and, just like that, you were officially a citizen of the world, or identified by a match. That is, unless you were a member of one of two castes of society. Occasionally, the very poor, living in remote locations, were not printed. Usually, the very rich, living in plain sight, also were not, simply because they had the wealth to avoid being printed along with the great unwashed. It was a status symbol to be unprinted.

No one in my family was printed except for me. I had to be because it was required when I became a police officer, although I wanted it done. Still, there might be hope of learning this girl's identity. I leaned against a squadcraft, already putting the case back in motion, based on Jana's news.

"We need to review all missing persons rep ..."

Jana stopped me, "I have. No one remotely similar has been reported missing who has not been accounted for in the state or surrounding states."

I thought of the effort my family made to let the world know we were trying to find Jack. It didn't work, but we tagged the I-net with reward offerings, also blogs, global police departments, even the library and mail systems. I reopened his case to no avail. I had looked at every John Doe brought in to the morgue if listed as Caucasian.

After seven years of viewing dead strangers, I found the faces began to be one, but never one like Jack's. Now here was someone that no one had reported missing, and she was a relative.

I looked at Jana, who waited for my instructions. With a little twist of history, the girl from the fill might have yet been standing somewhere under the same sky, hair shining, having a different conversation, having a life.

I thanked Jana for not sharing her findings with anyone. She agreed to let the report XO-BL3 disappear into her coded files for a few days until I told her what to do next. She wasn't quite through with me.

"Detective Edo, I want to do some other tests. I may still find out something really helpful."

"Jana, I am counting on just that."

I had my own idea where to look for answers.

7

I dropped into the port in front of the house. I always wondered how my mother arranged to keep each shrub and plant exactly as they had been for years. I asked her about it once, and her reply haunted me.

"I can't have Jonathan return and not recognize home."

My mother never used shortened forms of my name or Jack's. She had named me Kirtland for an ancestor, a Dr. Kirtland, in whose honor the Kirtland's Warbler had been named. I had read that the bird, rare even when it was discovered, had briefly flourished, but had not been sighted for eighty years and was presumed extinct. For all I knew, I was the last proof that the doctor, or the bird, ever existed.

By the time I got to the door, my mother was already waiting to embrace me, as if I had called before coming, when I had not.

"Kirtland, darling, it's wonderful to see you!" My mother threw her arms around me, then took my hand and led me through the white marble front hall into the living room. She talked as we traveled. "How is Suli? Why isn't she with you? Nothing's wrong?"

"No, Mother, Suli is fine. Have had a strange thing happen."

She turned to me.

"Let me look at you. My unflappable son, you look flapped. What is it?" Her face instantly altered as she read my eyes. "Is it anything to do with …?"

I stopped her gently before the sentence reached its inevitable last word.

"No, Mother, it's nothing about Jack. Let's sit. Where is Dad?"

"In the greenhouse, should I call him?"

"Yes, I need both of you to help me with something."

She paged him from the comunit at the couch. He came immediately. I stood to meet his customary bear hug.

"Kirt, what brings you out to the rustic little people in the countryside?"

"There is a twenty-something girl in the morgue, found in the NEAR, and her DNA indicates she is related to me, to us."

I was not prepared for my mother's reaction. She gasped, leaped up, and ran from the room. I turned to my father.

"Dad?"

He was looking at the floor, but slowly looked at me.

"Well, Kirt, you usually don't bring your work home, and you suddenly dropped that on us."

My gut twisted with a sick certainty.

"What do you know? Do you know something?"

"Give me a minute."

My father left the room and returned trailing my mother, who was pale and hollow-eyed. He settled her on the couch and faced me.

"We don't exactly know her, just of her. We got a call two months ago from a distant cousin, your mother's cousin, Grace Levitt. Her daughter Claire was missing. We wondered why we hadn't seen anything anywhere regarding it. She said they had been 'advised' not to report it, and there was no demand for money, just a suggestion that there was a good chance Claire would be returned. Claire even sent them a rambling note, postmarked in Spain, saying she was happy and she would come home after she did a bit more exploring. I think they are still waiting."

Fury overtook me and my voice flared.

"Why didn't you tell me? I could have helped! I'm actually in a position to help, to bring all kinds of help, and you kept this from me? Why?"

Suddenly, my mother wailed like an animal and began crying out. "You have to tell him, Quentin. Tell him!"

My father and I faced each other down, not a foot apart.

"We were warned after Jack not to interfere should anything like his disappearance occur again."

"What the hell?"

"You were eighteen. We had to decide if we should tell you."

I was breathing hard and took my father's shoulders in a vice grip. "Who the hell was the person warning you? They must know what happened to Jack, what happened to Claire, can't you see that?"

"Yes, but we had one child left to protect," my father said.

I reeled backward and went blind for a moment. I could only hear my mother sobbing. I shouted without thinking, "Congratulations, you got Claire to pay for me."

I threw myself away from them, and swept a flower arrangement off a table to shatter against the plate-glass doors to the back deck. It broke my anger. Silence.

I spoke in a voice I had never used with my parents before, a voice for the guilty, "You have to tell me everything. Maybe there were others before Jack."

Silence. I had made the three of us into strangers. I would count the cost later. Just then, only answers mattered.

"You can't protect me now. That's my job. I have to know why these, these people, whoever 'they' are, are targeting this family. Why?"

My father's voice matched mine, cold and objective. "They only take the potential heirs."

8

I shook my head as if to clear a place in my mind for an answer. "To what?"

"The NEAR, formerly called Long Landfill," my father responded.

Some part of me still hoped it was all a coincidence, but I had learned how to kill my hope before it could kill me.

"I'll shut up," I said, "Just tell me everything from the beginning."

Like some suspects, my father couldn't have stopped himself even if I asked him to.

"It once belonged to our family, beginning with my father, and four other families. About the time your mother and I married, the others sold their shares, but a few relatives of ours kept theirs, as we did. Even then, the landfill was a good thing to own," he explained.

"Shares became valuable beyond imagination," he said, "but not beyond greed. Someone wanted all the profit. The warnings started. You know how the fill is often in the news when fascinating or macabre things are found. The macabre things were messages, like that recent find of fingers in a jar of some liquid. We would get a strange call, telling us to pay attention."

I sat quietly, waiting. My mother did too.

"There was never any follow-up report, no one reported missing. It was to show the unfathomable wealth and power they had to make such things happen. Then ... Jack became the proof. We thought it was a mistake. Like you, Jack didn't even know we had ever had anything to do with the landfill. We still held a few shares, but not even one percent of the stock held. We couldn't imagine they felt threatened, but even one share was worth four hundred thousand credits when Jack disappeared."

My mother continued crying silently.

Dad went on, "We were contacted two weeks after he went missing and offered two options: sell the stock back into the corporation and declare no further familial claim to the Long Landfill."

My father stopped speaking, and a terrible softness came into his eyes. I waited, but he said nothing.

"What was the other option?" I asked.

"A message: There was a news story that night, showing dozens of silver candelabra found over time at the fill. They showed footage of how they found one very old one hidden in a barrel of flour. Among the items strewn in front of it was a bright red toy hovercar with a bent fender: your favorite toy when you were small. It looked like an innocent, discarded item, except, there were your initials, scratched in the finish," he explained.

It made sense, terrible sense. I waited for more.

"You may even have seen that report, but you were thinking about Jack then, and had no idea that you were in any danger. Only we knew the whole report was staged for our benefit, and they somehow had to have come right into this house to take that toy. They knew it was important to you as a child. They must have been watching us even then."

My father drove his next point home. "What you said about their taking Claire instead of you was cruel. We were only thinking of you."

I couldn't think of the words to take that back, but I moved to the couch and my mother came up into my arms and clung to me. My father seemed to have wound to a stop, but he took a breath and went on.

"Of course, we had to appear to be looking for your brother. We filed the missing persons report, offered a reward. You remember all the efforts we made. We couldn't have the police know what we knew. We had to call it a disappearance, not a kidnapping, or you would have been next. They could make that happen, whoever they were, whoever they are. I have kept a record of everything, dates, when and how we were contacted, the news reports, all of it, long overdue. I want you to take that information and do whatever you think is best. You are right, we can't protect you, but keep in mind you probably can't protect us, either."

He stopped, his voice returning to the voice I had grown up hearing at the dinner table, his face the face I knew, now damaged by another loss.

"Go, we have things to do. We have a plan in place. Kirt, son, we knew you would find out eventually, we just wanted to spend a little more time having you in our lives. Now, for all of us, that's impossible. They probably know you have guessed something. Claire was probably another message, but for whom?"

Wordlessly, my mother curled deeper in my arms and my father stood behind her and held us both. We stayed that way for a long time.

"I'll get that material. Kirt, I know you won't fail us, or Jack. You really are the only hope."

9

Suli watched me walk through the squad room. I was probably using my "thought walk," as she called it, when the windows could vaporize in a sonic blast and I wouldn't notice. I was also looking at her for all of the fifty yards that separated us. She waited like a queen until I stood before her.

"Kirt, I didn't know where you were. You always tell me, or at least log out from the system. You were AWOL, and I couldn't reach you. There must be some corporeal punishment for this. Water torture has always been my favorite. Just kidding. Okay, you are not amused. What's in the envelope?" she inquired. And tried again, "Suli to Kirt, I am at about sixty-two decibels, usually within the range of human hearing."

I moved around behind her console, pulled her chair back, and beckoned her to come with me. I looked neither left nor right, escorting her down the hall and out into the squad lot. The lot seemed to be part of my life now.

"Whatever happened to, 'Suli, I have this case, here are the reports, let's go over them.' Why are we out here?"

Suli looked at home under the sky as she always did. She shielded her eyes against the glare of the day and gazed at me, waiting. This was not going to be easy. I looked out over the city as I spoke.

"Has Jana shared anything with you lately?"

"She just said she was working on a special project, couldn't do a lot with my sad suicide, why?"

"I don't want you to ride with me for a while. There's a reason, a good reason. I might be able to tell you eventually."

Suli's hand dropped to her chest as if I had hit her. Her face went slack, but her voice never failed her.

"Kirt, did I do something wrong?"

"No, no, but I want you to tell the Chief it was your idea not to work with me for a few weeks. It can't appear to come from me. I want you to look angry, suggest I am being unprofessional, trying to undermine you or something."

Suli had become an alabaster mask. She looked at my badge as she spoke, "Well, no one will believe that, but I'm sure I'll think of something."

"Such as?"

She looked directly into my eyes.

"I might be able to tell you eventually."

She turned toward the door, and I tried to touch her arm, but she moved away from me at good speed.

"Suli ..."

She was inside, gone.

If anyone had watched that exchange, they would have had exactly the feeling I had: big damage done. I don't know what my face was doing, but I wanted to hit my head against the wall. God, I'd done that badly. Possibly it was just as well. I had to have her away from me to protect her. I was about to become something the department hates: a rogue cop.

Internal Affairs feeds on finding the officers who take bribes, run protection rackets, brutalize the public, act like vigilantes, pocket contraband, all the things we are hired to stop in the civilian world. It looks so much worse when it happens internally.

What I had in mind was misuse of police tactics and procedure, but I had about a half dozen reasons for doing it, a half dozen lives of the missing and murdered, as described in the envelope folded in my right hand. I had only skimmed the contents, but that was enough to warrant my actions, and I had to act alone.

I would be hampered, blind in the spot Suli covered, but I couldn't take Suli and her career down that road, in case I couldn't come back up that road. I still felt like shit for the way I had handled it. No help for it.

I lingered a few minutes in the heat of a spotlight day, feeling I deserved the punishment. I got back to the Cave in time to see Suli step out of the Chief's office and turn the opposite direction down the hall away from me. It didn't take three minutes for the Chief to call me in to pass sentence. Closed door: a pow-wow.

"Edo, Masters doesn't want to work with you anymore. She asked for reassignment to the 118th. Her reasons are confidential. You will spend three days at your station while we get you a partner. She will be on temporary duty somewhere, not here, until reassigned. Stay away from her, and get out of my office and out of my sight for the rest of your shift."

Whatever Suli had told him, it had worked well, too well.

I left the Cave and signed off from my photalk. I tucked the folded envelope deep in an inside jacket pocket. I headed toward my slipcraft, the envy of every one of my fellow officers, then veered toward the impound lot instead. If I was going to "go south," why not do it just a little sooner? Phil, the lot keeper, greeted me almost without looking up from his screen.

"Hi, Edo, what you need today? I got a great little Zip Craft we impounded for illegal nose-diving out by the mall. Sweet, worth looking at. So was the fifteen-something driver, great legs. Daddy will no doubt give her a talking-to and get her craft out any minute, so if you want to see it …"

"No time, Phil, I need to pull a nondescript 'anycruiser,' for a twenty-minute run. Maybe something we towed for illegal parking that no one is likely to pick up for a while. Have anything like that?"

"Well, can't you get an unmarked? Where's the autho?"

"No papers, Phil. No time, I've got twenty minutes, can't take my craft. Suli has the squadcraft, and I am burning minutes on a quick catch. Can you help me?"

"Edo, Mama taught me better, but I will do a surveillance clip and switch so there isn't any record of a craft going out. Be back in twenty minutes, or the view stays intact. Oh, and catch the guy, will you?"

"He has something I need for a case, so that's what comes back with me. Thanks, Phil."

"Don't mention it. To anyone."

He laughed, threw me a key card, and pointed to a real beater in the second row.

I pulled up quickly into a cruise lane, then shuttled through traffic pockets and dropped three to six levels at a time, to be certain no one followed me. At a corner deep in the shadow of first-level streets, I grounded. The mortally old building I approached had a blue light showing dully through a window. He was home.

His craft, if you could call it that, sat near the curb, leaning slightly forward at the passenger side, the rest strut bent. It was what we call a "cobblecraft" at the precinct, a vehicle pulled together from the ruin of other craft, with mismatched body parts. I knocked at a dark door, and a narrow sliver of face and body blocked the opening.

"I ain't done nothin', got nothin' to report, and you ain't welcome, Edo. You tryin' t' ruin me, comin' here?"

"Sniff, open the door. No one saw me come."

The face and body didn't move.

"Go away."

"Sniff, I will make noise, I will flash lights. It will be like Christmas out here."

The body turned the face and shambled back into the gloom.

"Fuck you, Edo. What do you want?"

The room was astonishing. Everything was brown: the walls, the sofa, the rug. It was like a mud hole except for the blue glow. It was emanating from the rarest of sources, a plasma TV, probably almost the last of its kind in a thousand miles. I was transfixed for a moment, watching figures shadow-dance across the screen. The plasma was so old it was only a whisper above gray.

"You're makin' me anxious, Edo. What do you want?"

The TV had by chance given me the perfect opening.

"There is only one place a man gets a TV like that, Sniff: the landfill auctions. Been to many?"

"I didn't steal it, if that's what you're gettin' at."

"No, I'll bet you actually bought it just as it is, a blue blur. When?"

"Two, three months ago, why?"

"When's the next sale?"

"Who knows? I ain't goin', got what I wanted."

"You are going to the next sale, Sniff."

"Why?"

"You are going to be my scout, to find out things for me."

Sniff rolled his rheumy eyes in the low light.

"You crazy? You tryin' to get me made? I'm just an itty bitty informant, but I show up askin' a lot of questions, look like I'm curious, someone will notice."

"No one will notice."

"Why me?"

"You've been to the sales before. You buy and sell things, you fix them. Your cobblecraft proves it. You have a reason to be there. Maybe you want to work there. I just want to know everything you can find out about the NEAR. Everything. What's more, I am going to pay you."

"Now you're talkin'. Good pay?"

"Yes, you'll be surprised. When can you start?"

"How surprised? How much?"

"Two hundred credits an hour. For that, you better have plenty to tell me."

The amount created an expression of greed on Sniff's face that almost lit the room. He tried to control it, but too late.

"Well, ain't perfect, but okay. Tomorrow night, Tuesday, I'll go. Sale's over 11 p.m. How do I let you know what I found out?"

"I'll find you."

"Pay me somethin' now, proof we got a deal."

I handed over a gleaming credit chip that magically disappeared on his person as if it had been an illusion played out in the half-light.

"Edo, you won't be disappointed."

I looked at my watch. Ten minutes until Phil turned me into a pumpkin, or just turned me in. I moved to the door and at the last moment locked eyes with Sniff.

"Results pay very well."

10

I got back to the lot with three minutes to spare, waving the envelope at Phil as I passed him. So far, smashing the rules was going entirely too well for me. I didn't want to think about how often Phil helped people to impounded craft.

Suddenly, I realized I had had a very long day. I had uncovered a terrible truth, forced my parents to dredge up a nightmare past, driven away a partner, and strayed into unethical territory, all before 6 p.m. Time to go home and think about my next move. I might have to involve the department, but the whole thing was so new. I wanted to ask Suli what she thought. Oh, hell.

I lifted my slipcraft out of the lot and headed northeast over the city to a gleaming glass tower. Twilight was spreading through the thicket of skyscrapers, and the sun shed a molten glow on the west side of my building.

Because I was used to it, my home seemed normal and right to me, but only two of my fellow officers had been to my place, Suli and my former partner Carl. It was largely because it was hard to explain or make light of the fact that I owned a penthouse on top of the most expensive real estate on the coast. Widely varying reactions made me wonder who should see the place.

Carl had walked in, whistled, and then asked for a beer. He unclipped his badge and draped his jacket over the end of the sofa. We sat down, Carl with his feet on the ebony coffee table before him, looking out at the city. He talked of work, drank his drink, and generally settled in as if the room were a big chaise lounge with a nice view. Not much fazed Carl. He could have been equally comfortable at Sniff's, as long as beer appeared.

Suli, by contrast, was transfixed when she came through the door. She could not turn away from the windows. I had to help her out of her coat, as her whole being was intent on seeing, not moving. I had been to Suli's home and understood the difference she felt.

For the past century or so, socioeconomic divisions had ceased to be horizontal and had become vertical. Cities, which had crumbled in the twenty-first century, had undergone a transformation. The cost of fuel had created an interest in a tight infrastructure, with food and services nearby, so cities became popular again.

The empty tall edifices became living places, with self-contained schools and businesses. Only the first to fifth street levels remained hopelessly poor, with even a few ancient automobiles nosing through the semidarkness at ground level. The switch to hydrogen fuel, drone and super-conductor technologies and meta-metals had set most vehicles free of the Earth.

Just when it was feared civilization would exhaust the oil supply, the new technologies had relieved the pressure on oil, and now the supply stretched into the foreseeable future. I understood from history that once the world had feared there would not be enough coal to sustain progress, but then oil had come forth, literally, to largely replace it. Now oil had been partially replaced, but people did not move back into the countryside, having rediscovered the value of "neighborhood" in the city towers.

We were still left with the fallout from the see-saw climate of recent years and the exponential growth of the human race. The carbon dioxide content in the air was improving, but was monitored. Some days, it was not safe to have an open-air sporting event. The athletes risked their health in an oxygen-poor environment, so the event would be moved to another day, or an indoor venue.

Suli lived at fifteenth level, a good level, in an apartment the size of my kitchen. She showed me around about two months after we had become partners, when we stopped to pick up a document she had left at home. The first time I saw her little world, I was as speechless as Suli was in my home.

Suli loved light. To get more of it, and to make up for the shadows cast by taller buildings, she had covered her ceiling with naturalights, enriched with good wavelengths for plants and people. The ceiling was the color of the sky, a rich blue, like the blue of a sunlit autumn day—a talisman against the coming gray of winter.

Suli also loved fresh air, so she decided to create that too, indoors. She took me on a tiny tour of her garden. Along the north-facing windows, she had planted a boxwood hedge in a continuous planter. A scattering of the miniature leaves fell into the soil beneath, tiny green confetti from a tiny green parade of bushes.

A royal palm leaned over the kitchen area. It was a young tree, the top of its trunk a smooth chartreuse vase sprouting a fountain of fronds. Suli had even built a grape arbor over her dining room table. The vines leaped up to explore and claim the wooden cross beams. The space came to life, with Suli as gardener and local goddess.

About six months later, Suli invited me over for dinner. She said it was to discuss an especially complex murder case. We had two suspects eminently qualified to be the killer, and we were looking for the one fact that would make us sure which one to push on the District Attorney's office.

I brought the wine. I had a bottle of one-hundred-year-old Para Vintage Tawny. I handed it to Suli at the door. She was wearing a silvery blouse, the sleeves pushed to her elbows. Her hair was drawn up in a bronze clip, with a few tendrils curling down the back of her neck. She looked at the label on the wine.

"Well, I see you have been shopping at the auction houses again, must have picked up this little item before the Picasso but after the Van Gogh."

"Parents' cellar, skipped the Van Gogh, and this probably tastes like prune juice by now. Open it. Let it breathe."

"And it will breathe so well in my apartment, thanks to the Plant People." Suli pulled the cork and tipped some of the contents slowly into two goblets. We sipped reverently and tasted the sun and rain of a century ago. Suli sighed with her eyes closed.

"Not a prune in sight. I do not know if my meal will be able to live in the same room with this wine."

"Let's find out. We can always throw the wine out or pour it on the plants."

"You are too well-mannered, but thanks for complimenting my cooking when you haven't tasted it yet."

Suli moved around her tiny kitchen as we talked about the case. She drew two filet mignons from the archaic broiler and placed them on two plates next to glazed carrots and some sort of dressed-up potatoes. We retired the five feet to the dining table under the arbor. Suli stepped back to the kitchen for a moment to draw the clip from her hair and shake it loose.

She touched the rheostat, which softened the light to late afternoon, and came to sit across the small table from me. The light swam down through the grapevines overhead, casting a shadow-leaf halo on Suli's hair. She looked at me with amber eyes, and smiled.

At that moment I couldn't have remembered my own name. I did try to follow her conversation during dinner, but I was impaled on her beauty. I am not sure exactly when it happened, but she had become beautiful to me. I think I commented on how delicious the meal was, and it was, but it could have been dirt and I would have eaten it just to stay at the table. At one point, she looked at me and laughed.

"You have had that last bite of steak poised on your fork for five minutes. You are in violation of a city ordinance if you don't eat it."

I raised the fork over my head like a sword swallower and lowered it to my open mouth to take in the steak with my teeth. I chewed, swallowed, and smiled hugely. She laughed again.

"That's more like it. Now, back to these two suspects: I like the store owner for this one, he had motive, had opportunity ..."

I dove into the conversation, because thinking about Suli made me uneasy. We had been partners for only about a year, plus, I knew I was not in a good place regarding how I thought about, or treated, women. They were like news reports. Those who were interesting enough at 6 p.m. were no longer news by the next morning.

That moment during the meal when I thought she was beautiful, I realized I was in trouble and decided I had to forget about how Suli "fit." I liked Suli: I didn't want more. I didn't *have* more for anyone, and especially not for a work partner, for God's sake. The job was challenging enough without that complication.

No, it was better to keep a great working partner happy than hurt a great woman. Only one thing threatened my resolve and that was Suli's way of being. How do you resist a way of being?

We parted that night with a hug at the door and our top suspect selected. She felt so small in my arms, damn, damn.

I headed toward home, but couldn't get enough distance from her embrace, or from my feelings. I swerved off to the north and landed on a lonely stretch of beach I knew well. The tide was out as evidenced by the lilting wave prints left by the receding ocean. There were bits of debris strung on the shore, but nothing valuable.

Kinseth's men would have gleaned such things for sale or use. Kinseth and his people had their camp nearby. His scouts were no doubt watching me from the line of sea oats at the top of the dune, but I knew it, and they knew me and kept the usual distance per his request. I took a pocketful of credit chips and stood them one by one in a line on the sand, my usual tribute. They would be gathered after I·left.

I funded several groups who supplied the essentials like mobile shelters and fresh water to the band of homeless people that lived just inland. Kinseth and I had an understanding. His people lived on this land I owned and would not be forced back into the cities. They fished and foraged as they wanted and were therefore some of the healthiest people on Earth and maybe a special sort of wealthy too.

Thoughts of them broke the Suli chain of thought but only for a minute. I lobbed stones and shells into the slow waves. There was usually comfort in being near the water. There was none that night. I wanted to think about Suli, and not think about her. I wanted a drink with the quiet backdrop of relaxed voices, not silent sentries awaiting my departure.

I made a short flight inland to an intimate bar I had visited a few times in the Hamptons. As one of the parking staff moved my slipcraft to a prominent space, another patron was landing.

The vehicle was a Laasn, and even in the dark, it drew attention. It was one sculpted long lick of midnight lacquer. Laasn was a Swedish firm that had delivered beauty and performance as conjoined twins in a line of lightcraft that cost over 550,000 credits for the basic models. This one was not basic. Neither was the woman who stepped down and allowed the reverent valet to place her craft in the center of the lot where every other guest could see it and despair.

I headed in just a minute before the other driver and took a seat at the long mahogany bar. I ordered a cognac. It arrived just as the owner of the Laasn entered the room and stopped a few feet from me.

I looked over casually to find her looking at me. She also was a sculpted presentation, from her motionless hair to her clinging blouse to her polished nails. The hard polish was even in her diction.

She asked, "May I join you?"

I was not going to be granted solitude, but I believed then, as I do now, that everything happens for a reason. I stood and pulled out the tall chair next to mine and seated her after she glided over as if motorized. She looked at my drink and smiled. I smiled.

"I'm having cognac. Would you like the same?" I asked.

"Which cognac?"

"Jenssen Arcana. A tablespoon could move the Earth off its axis if I poured it in the Amazon River, but I wouldn't want to waste any of it. Remy is milder. Would you prefer that?"

"I don't prefer anything mild."

The bartender had been hovering, only too glad to serve another expensive pool of heat in a glass.

We swirled our drinks for a moment and said nothing. The snifters cast off a scent of smoked spice and brimstone. We sipped and I watched for the inevitable, "Help, I'm burning!" look to fill her eyes. It didn't. She touched her tongue to one corner of her upper lip, and then practiced her perfect diction again.

"What fire are you fighting with this fire? The men I know have something like this not as an after-dinner drink, but as an after-disaster drink."

"I'm not one of the men you know."

"Kirt, of course you are! Just because you have been out of touch forever doesn't mean your original friends have forgotten about you. We miss you. I couldn't believe my luck when I saw you outside. I remember when you, Jack, and I used to meet at all the beach bonfires in the summer, along with Geena and Phillip and, oh, just everyone."

"That was years ago, Lizbeth. More than seven years ago."

"Yes, B.J."

"B.J.?" I asked.

"Before Jack. You were one of us before that terrible thing that happened to Jack. We could have been there for you, but you disappeared as if you moved to Tibet or something."

Jack's name in any conversation still hurt, but the constant drip of seven years had eroded the pain a little. The comfort of those friends I shared with Jack was not comfort to me, but I put on my pleasant face for Lizbeth, and my pleasant voice.

"I've never before had joining the police force equated with moving to Tibet, but it is a different world, so the comparison works."

My easy mood made her brave.

"Are you still a detective?"

Her tone made it clear she was asking if I might still be a leper. My tone made it clear that I was crusty with leprosy.

"Yes, I am."

She and the others had probably discussed what was good for me until they had the script memorized.

"As long as you stay a detective, you tie yourself to Jack. You need to move on, Kirt. Listen, I just stopped in here to get started on the evening. I am on my way to a fantastic party. You would know everyone there." She leaned in toward me and put her arm in contact with mine from shoulder to fingertips. Her voice came down an octave as her eyes half-closed. She touched the back of my hand.

"Come with me. We can get fantastically drunk and sleep it off somewhere together. I promise I'll be good."

She bowed her head for a moment and looked at me from the top of her eyes, and laughed. Three months before, I would have taken her up on everything, all of it, but something in me did a turn, like a wave on the beach rolling back to the good sea. I looked right at her. You usually sit at a bar to be next to, but not with, someone. I had been sitting at one kind of bar or another for seven years without knowing it until that moment. I spoke as gently as I could.

"I can't, Lizbeth, even given our shared history. I am involved with someone. I want to make it work with her."

She moved her arm out of touch. We both were silent, she because she was surprised, and I because I had, in three simple declarative sentences, stated my position on my past, my present, and my future. Lizbeth recovered first. She looked over my shoulder and around the bar, smiling, trying to lighten the moment.

"Are you hiding her in the slipcraft?"

I had to admire her style.

"No, just came from dinner with her. It's still new. I'm working on it."

She took up her snifter and we toasted each other before she finished her drink.

"Kirt, I am happy for you. You have moved on at last. Here, we can't have you buying drinks for any woman but your new love."

She opened her pointy little pocketbook and took out a thousand credit chip, which she clicked down on the bar. Her eyes shone a bit as she blew me a kiss and got down from her chair and left on her shiny shoes, returning to her Tibet. I put my own thousand credit chip next to hers and told the bartender to keep the change. We both smiled. Cognac even burns bridges.

I relaxed and savored the last of my drink before heading outside. The Laasn was still there, centered in the parking lot like a flawless gem in a setting of lesser stones. I could see Lizbeth through the windshield, engaged in conversation with a male passenger. She was animated, leaning toward him, while he looked out at me. *Didn't take her long to find a substitute for the evening's adventures,* I thought.

I reached my slipcraft and looked back to find him still staring my way, although I couldn't see him that clearly at that distance—older than Lisbeth, dark eyes, lean features, unknown to me but unsettling. Some people just have that look—good genes, bad motives.

I spent ten seconds mourning for Lizbeth and her future, shared with faces like his. Suli would give him the benefit of the doubt. I would be right in the end.

Forty minutes later, I ended up in front of Suli's door. I stood there for a long time, but I didn't touch the intercom, or knock. It was 2 a.m., and if she had come to the door with her hair tousled from sleep and her eyes soft, I would have downed her right there and burned away the darkness in love and want. But then I might have reconsidered in the morning. That would have ruined it, and us. No, everything had to be forward motion or not at all.

We had had dinner several times since then and had spent whole evenings just talking, but the ground rules stayed the same. Suli was, again, my most important case. That worked for me while I started over on being human.

11

I had to stop thinking about Suli. It hurt. I dropped onto the port on my roof and got out to let the craft settle under its recessed bubble cover. Through the translucent glass entry to the penthouse I could see the massive shadow of Clyde ranging back and forth eagerly.

My Scottish Deerhound almost flattened me every time I opened the door; no exception that night. I ruffled his fur and scratched behind his ears as he panted with joy.

"You can't fool me, you monster. You want to catch the scent of the nearest she-hound as much as greet me."

Clyde bounded past me, over the bubble cover and hit all the corners of the penthouse roof, but came to flex back and forth in a great gray half-circle around me. I let him dive and run and catch a ball for ten minutes, until he worked off some of his energy.

"Okay, let's see what you've done to redecorate the house."

We passed through the door together. There were the inevitable well-chewed shoes everywhere. Two corners of the Oriental area rug came up short of square, fibers in fuzzy trails on the floor. It wasn't bad. I left my shoes at the door, hoping the footwear junky had had his fix for the day.

I strode to the kitchen across the polished bamboo plank floors. Clyde leaped at the refrigerator, sliding to a stop with his nose on the freezer side door. I opened the other door and found the large bowl of spaghetti with meatballs. I speared a meatball with a fork and flipped it six feet skyward, where Clyde met it in midair. I gave him two more of the treats and heated some of the dish for myself.

The two of us sat and lounged on the living room rug, watching through floor-to-ceiling windows as the few taller structures lost the last of the light then gave off their own. Clyde crunched his way through a bowl of food, but I couldn't finish my meal.

I was hurting, and exhausted, and irrevocably changed. The day had been a battle with huge losses, of Jack all over again, and of contact with Suli and my parents. I wanted to look more carefully at what waited in the envelope I had thrown on the counter, but I knew rest would bring a fresh outlook in the morning. I had wanted to rush back to the precinct from my parent's house and "do something" immediately, but I knew that I needed to step back first and get my objectivity working for me.

I collected the envelope from the counter and took the few steps up to bedroom level. I put the envelope with my weapon and badge on the dresser and activated the night security system from the wall panel. I always imagined there was a hum when it ramped up from day coverage to total sensor level, but it was a silent changing of the guard.

A hot shower left me drenched clean. I hit the bed and felt fatigue pull me down like a G-force. Still, I didn't sleep immediately. Clyde loped in and took over the end of the huge bed in a mighty curl. I drifted in that middle place between knowing and forgetting, and finally slept, dreaming of a blue glow, lighting a hole at the bottom of the world.

12

I was awakened by Clyde launching himself from the bed toward the bedroom door. It was light. I surfaced from sleep to check the clock, only to see that it was almost nine, and I had never voiced on the wake-all. Clyde had heard our housekeeper at the door, and she was probably wondering why her key didn't work. The alarm system recognized her, but never allowed any key entry unless deactivated.

I could count on one finger the times I had overslept in my life. It wasn't such an issue, since I would be expected at my station and nowhere else. It was just proof of the toll yesterday had taken. Clyde had returned to be sure I was getting out of bed to greet his friend.

I'm not sure who was more surprised when I appeared at the door: Mrs. Albury or me. I was unshaven and had thrown on jeans and a T-shirt. We saw each other only occasionally, and never in the morning. I was always gone by the time she arrived. She came over twice a day, to clean, to let Clyde out, and to be his long-suffering plaything.

At our few meetings, she would recount his charming way of coming up behind her while she vacuumed, only to plant his front paws on her shoulders then fling himself around the apartment deliriously when she shrieked.

She was, thankfully, not a pushover at a solid five feet, four inches tall, and a hundred sixty pounds or so. It would take a seismic event to bring her down, and Clyde knew it. I knew she liked him, secretly—very secretly. I was far less sure how she felt about me, but she kept Clyde from demolishing the house.

Everything that could be cleaned, was. A scent of windswept forest lingered in the rooms after she had been here. There were houses that actually cleaned themselves, and robots to care for animals, but I took a kind of comfort in the idea that a real person was breaking up the day's monotony for Clyde, and that real hands fed him and put the house right. Mrs. Albury was a treasure, arriving every weekday in her tiny hovercraft, which was so small she almost wore it rather than operated it.

After our initial awkwardness at the door, my housekeeper eyed me curiously, returned my "good morning," and headed right for the kitchen, where Clyde had beaten her to the refrigerator door. I went back to my bedroom to shower and shave. I was surprised to smell coffee as I picked up my gear from the dresser and walked into the sunlight of the main room.

Clyde was chewing on an old-fashioned mop handle. Mrs. Albury knew how to divert him from her real cleaning tools. There was a steaming mug perched on the marble countertop, next to a plate of eggs and sausage.

In the history of breakfasts, it was a standout. I was hungry and thirsty, but it did more than satisfy the body. The simple actions of Mrs. Albury moving through the apartment humming and Clyde lolling next to the mop, taking a break, restored some sense of order and beauty to my damaged world. I felt the way you feel when you are eight, family is present and accounted for, and the future has only shown its promise, not its teeth.

I found Mrs. Albury folding laundry. I meant to thank her, but in a completely unplanned moment, I took her hands and thanked her for breakfast. She colored slightly and said it was nothing. I think we both felt otherwise.

I shrugged into my holster, ready to start the day. Clyde shadowed me. He knew the routine, but as I patted him before closing the door behind me, his look told me I owed him the usual weekend run at the park for this abandonment during the week. I always paid my debt. Often, Suli joined us. I didn't know when that would happen again. I narrowed my focus to the coming day.

The Cave was subdued. Suli's desk was neat and empty. Everyone avoided looking at me as I passed them, so I knew the word was out: I had somehow driven away one of the squad's greatest assets. Partners argued. They didn't part, except for extraordinary reasons. I knew I was generally liked, but that was always tempered by a little distance. Now the distance was king.

There was a message on my private comline. I tried to quell my hope that it was from Suli until I found it wasn't. It was from Jana. She simply said she would be out at a forensics conference for the day, but hoped I would meet her after four at the FAcility where they had taken the LastSteel dome pieces from the fill. There was no hint of emotion, or that dreamy quality, either—sure signs Jana was not herself.

The Speedict unit sat before me on my desk, seeming to accuse me of having nothing to report. Some of the detectives dictated reports, but I found it was usually easier to type and let the unit correct and condense the report. Verbal dictation still had to be verbally edited while swimming in a net of conversations in the room, which seemed more tedious to me.

To the unit's right was a stack of documents, deskwork from hell. Whoever believed we had a paperless society was welcome to come and take care of this for me. The heap ranged from reports with some incidental information missing, to files on rape kits that were backlogged for processing.

You would think DNA printing would make rapists easier to prosecute, but defense lawyers had risen to meet the challenge of good evidence by flooding the system with clearance requirements and rights documents, all of which had to be processed by people, not "robotic intervention," due to the gravity of conviction: castration.

It could still take months or even years to file everything needed for processing the tests. A wall of paper could still stand between victims and justice.

I first waded in on the rape kits. There was real value in that. Two hours got me through one complete case. I needed a break, so I went outside to try to call my parents. I used my Blade, which encrypted calls and was still the standard for safety seven years on.

No answer on the house line. They each had unlisted PersoNet numbers, but I was reluctant to call either of them. There would be a record when a call was placed, even if the content was protected.

My father's envelope was again in my jacket pocket. All my training told me to go to the commander with it, but my instincts said otherwise. Why? I trusted my fellow officers, but there is a limit to trust without absolute proof that it is deserved. I absolutely trusted only the person I absolutely couldn't consult.

I surprised myself by my reluctance to bring the department resources to bear on this potentially huge case. I told myself it was caution. I reasoned that for Claire and Jack action would already be too late, so they could wait another day until I got more information from Jana and Sniff. Also, I didn't want to expose my family without enough reason to do so.

The day wore hard. I could safely say I had ironclad paperwork on four rape kits. No one spoke to me until about two when Ken Dunne casually walked up to me and asked if he could look at one of the reports. He took the top one and appeared to read it with interest, but he spoke softly as he turned the pages.

"Suli is out at the Public Relations office in Five Points. I don't know the whole story, Kirt, but I figure there are two sides to everything. I would guess the next move is up to you."

"Thanks, Ken, and thanks for the stay of execution."

He smiled quietly and strolled off down the hall. Things got nearly back to normal after that, or as normal as a truce allowed.

I headed out to meet Jana at 4:15 p.m. I had one stop to make on the way, but I arrived about 4:30.

The LastSteel dome had undergone an amazing transformation. In its cleanroom with glass walls, the dome wore color-coded dots with stripe codes attached to its interior and exterior surfaces, each next to possible evidence: a smear, a speck, a hair, something.

There were so many dots it looked like an outbreak of some freakish LastSteel pox. Next to it on the floor was the silicone that had been removed from the cut edge of the dome, and also from around the girl's, Claire's, body. I couldn't be positive it was Claire, but I felt it was.

The silicone could be highly useful as it would have picked up information in beautiful detail from every surface it touched, down to the pore pattern of skin. It was spread out like a giant clear skin itself. More dots were there, and sections were missing, carved away in squares and circles.

The facility was relatively deserted, since it wasn't on what you would call a highlight of the city tour. *Here, ladies and gentlemen, is the FAcility, the Forensics Annex, the place where big things go after they die, and sometimes little things, like people.*

There was room to reassemble mass hovercraft wrecks with the vehicles in the exact positions they had occupied in the sky just prior to impact: the climax of a ballet frozen in time, where no one danced away at the end.

A rabbit warren of rooms, full of forensic equipment, surrounded the huge central space. You did not go into any of them unless you were asked.

I was still looking at the dome when I heard a familiar voice behind me.

"Jane Doe is not here. She is at the morgue." It was Jana. She walked up quietly to stand next to me. "I thought we would be less conspicuous over here. The Cave has big ears."

"Good thinking, Jana, since I haven't spoken to anyone at the department yet. Or is there another reason, something you found?"

She didn't answer immediately, but looked around us. No one was within sight, but she moved off toward the west side of the building, and I followed. We passed two people watching reports on vieunits who didn't even look up, but simply swerved around us in slow motion as they walked in the other direction.

We stepped into a room with sleek black tables under recessed lights. The missing cutouts from the silicone rested in pans, looking like stranded jellyfish paralyzed by the glare. Jana touched the switch on a round device the size of a layer cake. It began to emit a soft white noise, a constantly drawn breath that soothed the mind.

"I tell them I like the sound," Jana said. "It helps me think. It allows me to make verbal notes all the time I'm working, but it interferes with the surveillance audio. We need that now."

She looked down into one of the pans. "The girl was killed by a lethal injection of so many drugs it doesn't matter. Someone just poured a brew of poisons together, when any one of the ingredients would have dispatched her instantly. It's as if it couldn't happen quickly enough. It was done either by someone who couldn't have cared less, or someone who didn't want her to suffer."

Jana moved to a particular slice of the silicone and suggested I look closer. The shining surface threw back distorted reflections, but I couldn't see anything unusual. Jana leaned in and pointed to minute specks on the surface as she spoke.

"There were microscopic spores, plant pollen, and bits of leaf matter and grass imbedded in the skin of her feet, which the silicone lifted. She must have been walking barefooted sometime just prior to death. But there was no dirt, not one particle. How do you pick up that kind of plant matter without any dirt?" Jana speculated.

"Someone cared very much about the girl's appearance," she went on. "She is intact, less the ring finger. Maybe she was wearing a ring so tight they couldn't remove it, so they sacrificed the finger. But why not just cut off the ring if they had the strength and the tool to cut off the finger? It doesn't make sense."

Jana sighed, like the white sound. "One thing is certain. This was staged. I read your initial notes about finding her at the bottom level of the fill. The LastSteel dome is old, but certainly not a hundred and fifty years old, meaning they had to move the dome with the girl in it from some other location to that location, which is very deep in the fill and therefore very old."

As I considered the logistics of that move, Jana said, "How could that be done without someone noticing? There are ScanEyes everywhere, the robots are recording all the work that is done, yet there is nothing on the surveillance as per our robotic scan. Someone altered all that. Who?"

Who indeed, I wondered.

"I know you want to pursue this, Detective Edo, but I have to tell you what I think. I think this was staged for you. What are the chances that you just happened to be the one nearby to take the call? Add that to the odds of your being related to the girl, and also that your partner just happened to be called to some other case so you were alone at the scene, and you have a pile of coincidences as high as that landfill."

She leaned against the table and momentarily looked at the ceiling, as if there were answers written there.

"There is something else," she said. "I have a dead girl at the morgue and a LastSteel dome the size of a small transport sitting in this building, and there has not been one inquiry from the precinct about it. Talk about the elephant in the middle of the room! How could there not be one question about this from anyone, except you? There hasn't even been an inquiry about why there isn't any official report from me. I think someone very high up in the precinct is part of this."

Her theory hung in the room, the white sound a prolonged gasp echoing around us. Jana wasn't finished. She went on in a voice that had developed a tremor the white noise couldn't hide.

"I have such a strong feeling about this that I did something this morning before I left here. I flipped the breaker on the ScanEye, so we have not been seen. I will leave it that way until someone notices, which could take a day or two. I must have used my last courage on that act of defiance, because I am, now, afraid."

Her voice was almost a whisper, so that the last word dropped out in the middle, and became "afr----d."

"Detective Edo, someone has such power to do something like this, such resources. It feels like a trap."

I had to think of how to reassure her, while hiding my own feelings. I stood next to her and put my arm around her shoulders. She was trembling.

"Jana, think about it, go to the next step. If someone wanted you to discover all this, and that the girl was a recent homicide, you did exactly what was wanted. They're ecstatic. They will probably send you a reward."

Jana allowed herself an experimental smile as I continued, "But that would be bribery, so to keep you out of trouble, I did some special work at my desk today. I had the same feeling you have. I drilled through the socket layers between my computer and your initial reports and notes and removed your name. Now the file on Jane Doe XO-BL3 was prepared by Kirtland Warbler."

Jana giggled nervously.

"Seriously, Jana, don't worry, I did something else, too. I changed some of your findings and indicated the body was old, so with no point in further investigation, the case is closed and therefore unlocked and viewable. I put a subliminal tracker on the report. If anyone accesses it, I will know who it is. A trap for a trap, what do you think?"

She looked up at me with large eyes. She was processing the concept.

"Oh, I see. When they see the report, and that signature, they will know you know what is happening. But what if they do something else even worse, now that they have your attention?"

"What they wanted was my attention, Jana, and they will like that I have not gone public. Now, they will have to contact me somehow. That's just what I want. If they wanted to kill me, I wouldn't have been here to have this conversation."

Jana nodded.

"When this is all over, Jana, I can tell you some things about this case I have learned from some sources of mine, but for now, the less you know, the safer you are. Speaking of safety, I would like you to have a family crisis you need to attend to in another state."

I knew I had her attention at that.

"My lousy office job does give me access to all kinds of documents, such as leave-of-absence requests. As a glorified clerk, I can make you gone, with pay, for up to two weeks. There is an old saying about never underestimating the power of a clerk, and now I know how true it is," I explained.

"Use cash, take a trip. They are not interested in you, but let's just be cautious. It's all arranged, actually. Don't even go home, just take off from here and rent a craft in a nearby city. Don't take your own. This is a tempcard in a false name, with great false credentials, loaded with thousands of credits paid for with cash. It can't be traced. I bought it, and the creds, at a hologram arcade. I have learned some useful things from criminals about how to travel well."

Jana wasn't sure what to say. She tried to protest about the tempcard, although I assured her that was not a worry, but didn't explain why. I knew she was relieved, although she didn't say so. That would have been acknowledging that she might be in real danger, and we weren't going to talk about that.

We walked toward the front door and parted out in the vehicle lot at her craft. Jana promised to go on a shopping spree for everything she needed and then disappear. I turned to her just before leaving and took her hands, which were very small, and cool, but not cold with fear.

"Jana, the white noise, the surveillance shutoff, that was good thinking. You might want to get into police work, become a detective."

She gave a slight, shaky laugh.

"No, thank you! Give me nice, quiet evidence that speaks only when it is commanded to do so. But thank *you*, Detective Edo, for everything."

"My name is Kirt, Kirtland the Warbler, remember that."

She hugged me, then waved as she lifted away into the afternoon.

I had completed four rape cases, protected Jana, and resurrected an extinct bird, all in just hours. Not bad for a clerk.

I returned to the precinct to finish out the day. More reports had magically appeared on my desk. I joined the drone of the room, tapping out notes and sometimes dictating, which is the way to become invisible in plain sight.

Just before closing down the files, I logged quietly into the doctored report on the landfill case. It hadn't taken them long to come visiting. There were two hits. I opened the log. One was from the office of the Chief, which could be an assistant, but I was guessing it was the man himself. It could be due diligence, either checking on the progress on cases, especially a case that apparently parted two of his best detectives, or it could be more than that.

The other hit was Suli.

13

I sat staring at her ID code, not moving. I closed my eyes for a moment. Suli? She could have the same reasons to access the report as the Chief. All the same reasons. What if?

I knew one thing: These faceless and still nameless people had me doubting my most-trusted ally, and I hated them almost as much for that as I hated them for Jack and Claire, and the others. I didn't know yet what they wanted with me. This was not their usual method of operation. There had to be a reason they were "waiting and baiting."

I headed home, and after my greeting ritual with Clyde and a quick meal, I sat at the counter and slid the envelope contents out onto the cool marble counter. The material was organized in a timeline from Jack's disappearance to the present.

Most of it consisted of old holographic chip reports about Jack, but there were chips that had question marks on the labels, along with a person's name, as if my father wondered if they were part of the pattern of disappearances or accidents, or not. I noted all names to cross-reference against NEAR owners.

One example was a report on a debutante, killed when she smashed her slipcraft into a commuter span on her way to her eighteenth birthday party. The craft was on autopilot, which could not, by definition, fly her into any object. Nothing was found to be wrong with the programming.

I focused on the reports regarding things found at the landfill. I played several of them. One was on the jar of fingers, which my father had mentioned. Of course, Claire's missing finger. I immediately guessed her parents were warned to look for the report, and I imagined their horror, realizing they could not know if it meant Claire was dead or if it was to reinforce their silence.

We at the police department would certainly have collected that jar as evidence, but might not have DNA-tested the contents yet. I would pursue that, and visit Claire's parents, a dreaded task. I also played the report that showed my childhood toy. It was strange to see it there, meaningless to an entire world full of people except for three of us.

Well, Sniff would be at the landfill sale that night, so I would find him tomorrow and get whatever information he could add. I could also make a follow-up visit to the fill, ostensibly to close out the investigation.

Possibly Reeves and Corzo knew something. My gut said they knew nothing, but were following orders. I would probably have a new partner to take with me on this trip, but it didn't matter. I would get what I wanted: another look, another chance to ask questions.

Clyde, who had been lying next to my chair, suddenly lifted his head from his paws and looked toward the front doors. An instant later, both of us were standing as someone's shadow fell across the frosted glass. I pushed everything into the envelope as the comunit at the door activated.

"Kirt, it's Suli. I need to talk to you."

Any other time, her voice would have been so welcome. Now, I hated the fact that I wondered why she was there. What if? I hesitated. Once there was no glass between us, my objectivity would be impaired. I had to risk it. Was she the messenger? I only knew I was on the way to let her in because I had to have her before my eyes, whatever the price.

As the doors slid open, I was prepared for anything, I thought. I wasn't prepared for the way she looked. The door lamps cast a soft light that didn't help at all. Suli appeared wretched. Her eyes were red-rimmed. Her chestnut hair was unkempt, breaking up the blue halos of light that usually shone in it. She was dressed in a light jacket and old jeans and a navy T-shirt. I was blindsided by the urge I had to pull her to me to stroke her hair and protect her, but what right did I have when I hadn't even called her?

I stepped back to allow her in, and she passed me wordlessly. She put out her hand to stroke Clyde's head, then walked slowly to the north-facing windows and stood with her back to me. She said nothing for a minute or more. It seemed up to me to speak.

"I meant to call you." It sounded off-hand and cruel. I instantly tried to fix it. "I have been on desk duty from hell. There are some problems with … my family. A lot of things are strange right now. I'm sorry I didn't call."

She spoke without turning.

"I know that, basically, there is only one reason a man doesn't call. He doesn't want to call. With a world of instant communication where you can literally call someone from the space station, the person on the space station still has to want to call."

Her voice had lost its brightness and speed. Her words barely moved and struggled to cross the distance between us.

"I waited," she said. "I was sure you would explain things quickly. I didn't even mind terribly coming up with an explanation for wanting to transfer, but you didn't call. So I looked for reasons, if you weren't going to provide them. I am a detective, after all. I saw you take off in an unmarked. I went into your reports this afternoon and saw the one about the Jane Doe at the landfill. It was completed, but a friend at the precinct said you went out to the FAcility, and a friend there said you met Jana."

One of the people who passed us in the hallway, I thought.

"Then I heard that you met Jana out in the squad lot yesterday, before you asked me to get lost."

"I didn't ask you to get lost, I …"

"You know what I mean."

The idea that I was being watched by not only the unknown entities but also known ones started to bother me, a lot. Slow anger was in my mind, but I kept it out of my voice.

"Suli, ask what you want to ask, don't circle the issue. Ask me what you want to ask, and if I can answer, I will."

She exhaled, hard, and looked at me with broken eyes.

"You have had every chance to connect with me, but

you never take the chance. You're seeing Jana. She doesn't like that you ride with me, so you wanted to change that for her."

The relief was so great that I actually forgot that her take on my behavior probably made a lot more sense than what was really causing my behavior. I blurted out, "What?" and started to laugh. Wrong reaction.

Suli went absolutely white, but her white was not the color of fear. She leaned forward slightly from the waist, fists clenched, eyes sparking. Clyde stepped backward to watch us from a safe vantage point, his head cocked to one side. Suli had her voice again.

"How can you laugh? I have been devastated, you, you idiot!"

"Suli, wait, let me explain! It's not what you think at all! It would take first prize at the not-what-you-think awards. This, this has nothing to do with Jana. She was just helping with this landfill case. That is all, all of it. I can't blame you for wondering, but the problem is that I can only tell you what it is *not*. I still can't tell you what it *is*, not yet. Only I swear it has nothing to do with Jana. I know more about … the moon than I know about Jana."

I don't know where the moon comment came from, but for some reason it was what I said in the heat of the moment. Suli seized on the one thing in my words that seemed to relate to another woman.

"You don't know anything about the moon, so that is a stupid comparison."

I searched my memory frantically, while trying to keep this argument on track.

"It has a crater named Tycho, and, hell, something else. The point is that I don't care about Jana. Suli, until these last few minutes, we have had the most incredible ability to understand each other. I know it's my fault that you don't know what's happening, and I am so sorry for that, so sorry that I hurt you. I promised I would tell you eventually, remember? I absolutely will tell you everything. It is just that I need a little more time."

I had moved closer to her. I so wanted that underlying unity back between us. I had broken it. I had to fix it. We were only two feet apart, looking into each other's eyes. My next words might be the most important of my life. I tried to take myself out of those words and make them only about her.

"Suli, you are *the* woman. You are not just my partner. You are my ally, my best friend, my confessor. I haven't even explored all the things I feel about you because I know now that I'm damaged by my anger over the loss of my brother. I haven't had any relationship of value with a woman in seven years, except ours, and I'm working on it. I just wanted it to be perfect."

She was looking at me as if I were a stranger. *Not a good sign,* I thought. She spoke haltingly at first, her voice breaking.

"It isn't perfect. I am not perfect. You are not perfect." Suddenly she picked up speed, and anger. "Let's think about what I want this time. I want to wreck this relationship, or anyway, the one you've built. I want a real one, with accidents and mistakes in it, and damage and forgiveness, and … everything."

She closed the distance between us and kissed me hard on the mouth, then slapped me quickly, then kissed me again. The second kiss was the One. She tasted of tears, and mint. We didn't stop that kiss while I helped her shed her jacket. She kicked off her shoes. Clyde had at them.

Suli broke the kiss and instead ran her hands up my chest underneath my shirt. I pulled it off to get it out of the way for her. Hers came off next. She crossed her arms to get it over her head. I had my first look at her body set free, stretching upward, with her hands lifting and her head thrown back to shake her hair loose. My life shook loose with it. I closed in to connect with her, but she pulled back for just that last moment, her eyes filling, her voice swooning.

"I wanted to be wearing something beautiful when this happened, not these clothes ..."

"I don't care."

"Ohhhh, I didn't shave my legs ..."

"I don't care."

I caught her to me again as her lips shaped a word. She never said it. We swam and throbbed through a haze of touching. We stripped each other. We shed everything, everything that separated us. I got her to my bed somehow, to our bed. Wet. Deep. Breaths. Cries.

Time fell victim to us and stayed and stayed. The months of denial were the best foreplay. My hands bent her body to me, her legs spreading and clinging and rocking. Suli's skin impacted mine, bringing with it her scent and imprint, invisible, yet more real than anything visible. She moved against me, and with me, to a soaring climax. We did not let ourselves fall away from each other's bodies for even a moment, until sleep and gravity left us next to each other in matching peace.

We touched each other awake at 6:00 a.m. Clyde had decided to reclaim a portion of the bed, but it was so spacious he looked at us and yawned from a spot below Suli's feet: a certain sign she was accepted. He rolled off the bed and trotted out of the room.

Suli curled near me and we didn't move for minutes. I told her then that we needed to continue the charade of separation at work because what I was working on could be dangerous for her in a way I couldn't explain. She tried to protest. I kissed her into silence. I promised her I would keep her informed of my whereabouts, and this thing that had happened between us was just the beginning.

When I told her I had sent Jana away for her own safety on some trumped-up emergency, Suli spooned up against me. Her movements tied us into a love knot that took a while to untie. We didn't hurry.

We showered together and I marveled at her in full light. She had a faint bruise on her thigh. I kissed it. That little bruise helped make her real while we were avoiding flawlessness. Suli ran her hands over me, trailing soap across my shoulders. She held me away from her to take a deep look. She did not speak. She smiled, though, a slow, curvy smile.

As we dressed we would have looked like any newly minted couple forged from a mix of hard-earned love and unparalleled sex, except for the lasermagnum I strapped on under my coat.

There was condensation on the windshield of her hovercraft and a light fog surrounded us in a rooftop world of half-dawn. We held each other amid the morning sounds of our time, as lovers had held each other since man discovered love, hopeful for the new day.

We agreed I would call her, without fail, sometime after lunch. Just before she lifted away, Suli smiled slyly and gestured for me to lean in to hear her over the whine from the lift engine.

"You and Clyde owe me a new pair of shoes. These used to be close-toed."

We kissed before she cruised off into the hum of the city.

14

The squad room had never been less inviting. The others moved around the room as usual, but with a sliding glance or a smirk from a few of them. It was easy to see why. There was a new tenant at Suli's station. *They wasted no time acquiring someone,* I thought.

He looked eager, every part of him. He sported a spiky brush cut, so his hair was at attention. His suit was dark blue and crisp as a candy wrapper, and fit him about as well. He had freckles, even on the backs of his hands. They had assigned me a rookie so new he practically squeaked.

He leaped out of his seat as I approached. He must have asked how he would know me when I arrived. I wondered what they told him. "Edo? Six-two, dark hair, wears a lasermagnum, young for a detective."

"Hello, Detective Edo, I'm Brian Shand, uh, Officer Shand. It's an honor to meet you. They brought me over from the 118th, I'm just about to enter the PUSH Program, but they said I could do paperwork for you, maybe be helpful, since your partner is away, or whatever."

He finished lamely, as if he had been told something else about Suli, but didn't want to say it. He put out his hand and I shook it. He had a firm, sincere grip. Either he had been taught a handshake had to be firm, or he was the kind of person who just was that way. You can teach the handshake, not what underlies it.

So what was this kid doing here and why was I thinking of him as a kid? He was probably only five or six years my junior. There had to be a detective available to work with me temporarily. I couldn't be certain, but I felt he was either assigned to me so he could report back to someone, or this was a novel punishment for losing Suli. Whichever it was, I was about to make his life interesting, because a rookie might fit my plans perfectly.

"Good to meet you, Brian. You can call me Kirt. You probably know I am not officially assigned to any cases right now, but if you want to look at this as an opportunity to do some police work, we'll be fine. I'll take you with me this morning, and I'll leave you here this afternoon, part field work, part station work, pretty much a typical day in the Cave."

"Cave?"

"We call this the Cave, old holo-equipment, mostly older personnel."

He looked happy to be told something insiders knew.

"Whatever you say. Hey, they said it was fine if I wore a suit instead of my uniform so I could blend in a little better with you guys."

"Good idea. Our first stop is the NEAR. I have some last questions on a case that is basically closed."

We walked out to the squad lot. I motioned for him to pilot. He seemed to grow an inch taller as he straightened his jacket and walked to the left wingdoor. We strapped in and lifted off to a height of fifty feet or so. He looked at me.

"Which way?"

He had passed one test. If he had known the route without asking, I would have had a clearer idea who was riding with me. He could be the devious guy who hides behind that "Who, me?" look, but my instinct told me he was not.

We reached the fill in twelve minutes. Officer Shand piloted like a man who was remembering everything he learned in class, recently. He reached to the combutton to notify dispatch where we were going, but I stopped him. He looked at me without speaking, waiting a moment, then went back to his piloting.

"I want to arrive without prior warning. The person I want to interview may be more forthcoming if he hasn't been coached by someone first."

Brian looked puzzled.

"But I was calling dispatch, how would that warn someone outside the department that we were coming?"

"I have reason to believe someone at the precinct has something to do with events that happened at the NEAR."

I looked for a sidelong glance, an unconscious reaction to being told what he already knew, a reaction he would try to hide. Instead he turned to me with slightly widened eyes.

"Wow, are you serious? Are you going to report it to Internal Affairs? I mean, I would understand if you didn't want that known, everybody hates the investigators from IAD. Um, I guess I shouldn't have said that. Sorry, eyes ahead."

He looked so flustered I laughed.

"Brian, don't worry about it, I'm not reporting to IAD, yet. Go ahead and call dispatch and tell them we are headed to the Library of Records, and we will go there to get an original document for a rape kit. Let's call this thing right now a side investigation, part of a closed case, cleanup work, which is appropriate for a landfill. It won't take long."

He looked relieved.

"I guess you're sort of coaching the rookie, right?"

"Something like that."

The pretty secre-tech at the main building was the most voluptuous, buxom young woman I had ever seen. She somehow conjured up images of a parade balloon figure that needed handlers to keep it from drifting into a light post. Brian couldn't keep his eyes off her.

She called Tom Reeves at my request and went back to pushing data with her finger stylus. I hoped she wouldn't somehow puncture herself with the stylus and deflate. Brian might never recover.

Reeves did appear. He did not smile, and his voice held no welcome, or interest.

"What a surprise. What was your name again, officer?"

"Detective Edo, and this is Officer Shand."

"I remember now. How are things with the dead girl?"

"I'd like to ask a few questions, take a look at the scene again."

"I really didn't have that on my schedule today, detective and officer. Could you drop in unexpectedly another time when it might be more convenient, or not?"

"If we do this my way, Mr. Reeves, everything can go on as usual, no need to stop any work being done. If we do this your way, I get a court order to halt all work, and a search warrant, and bring lots of time-consuming investigators over for the day, or longer. Your choice."

The luscious secre-tech stopped filing data and looked over at Reeves, wide-eyed. Brian stood absolutely still. Reeves tried to stare me down, then flinched.

"You swing that badge pretty hard, don't you, detective? So, is it the grand tour, or what? Your choice."

I asked Brian to remain behind, to possibly glean some information. He didn't look unhappy with his options, after stepping outside into the landfill-scented air. Reeves and I walked to a Masher in the lot and he set it on autoguide to the fill entrance while we suited up in the airlock. With helmets tipped back, we moved to the control panel to look at the tunnel strung out ahead like a canopy road under street lights.

The haze and sense of closeness in the fill were exactly as I remembered them, iced with the undisguised hatred of Reeves standing at the controls, next to me. I ignored it. I had been hated before, and by better haters than Reeves. I spoke over the rumble of the Masher treads.

"Is there a command center in the fill, a place where all information is processed?"

Reeves pointed to his chest.

"Right here, I run it all, from my office, or from any of the Mashers. I have priority-voiceover on all the comunits. I can call in data and pass it through any control panel. Why?"

"I was expecting to see something on the surveillance that wasn't there, that had to be there."

I wasn't going to tell him I had expected some image of the LastSteel dome being moved to the spot in the fill where it was "discovered." Since talking with Jana, I had asked for a total search of the surveillance for the last four years, had directed the viewbots to look for it, and it simply wasn't there. Somehow, that image had been lifted, or there was another path to the fill face that had no coverage.

Reeves just looked ahead, adjusting our trajectory down the tunnel.

"Well, maybe you screwed up. Whatever you were looking for, if it wasn't on the record, is your problem. We gave you everything. We cooperated fully. Anyway, what's the difference? She was dead, dead, very very dead, and long dead. Guess she screwed up, too."

He looked over at me and smiled. Either he didn't know anything, or he knew everything. He had given me another angle of attack.

"You mentioned the comunits, that you can break in, listen in, override, what?"

"All of that. We record everything—well, not this little scenic trip we're taking, no point. The only thing I can't do is delete. What, you want the audio now, too? You can have it. Comunits are so important here that we re-invented them, making them durable, movable, and traceable. I bet you high school graduates with your love of petty authority think you cornered all the great technology. Try this with any of your toys."

As I watched, he walked to a side panel and flipped it open to reveal rows of spare comunits. Reeves scooped out two of the dime-sized mesh buttons. He popped two in his mouth and sloshed them around, and spit one out into each hand.

He pressed on each of them once to activate them and said a long sultry "hellooooo" into the gold one, the sound trailing out of the silver one in a metallic replica. He stuck them to the console, then scooped them up, pressed each of them twice to turn them off, and tossed them at the wall, where they attached themselves instantly. He laughed raucously.

"Surprises the shit out of the new hires."

I didn't let his little show stop me.

"Do all workers have them?"

"All the human ones, yeah. We try not to lose people in here. The comunits even have G dots in them, because we discovered some people get disoriented in the tunnels once they're outside the Mashers, so even if they could contact us if they had trouble, they couldn't tell us where the hell they were. Made them a little nervous."

He said it with contempt, as if losing such workers wouldn't really matter.

"The comunits are really tiny 'black boxes,' like the old passenger jets used to carry. One receives, one transmits, they even sense the units nearby so a team of workers can communicate easily. On a broader scale, we can know everything the person has said or heard that day if we want. We can recover everything ever said or heard if we want. We have a tight little kingdom under the ground here."

He looked me up and down slowly. "You don't like enclosed spaces, do you, detective? I can always tell. Only the phobiacs ever care about tracking or comunits. We weed them out right away."

"I'm standing here with you, with forty stories of trash over my head, when I could have questioned you in the fresh air."

"Okay, detective, maybe you're not a phobiac, maybe that expression you're wearing just indicates you can't wait to get out of here so you can shower. You can think you're better than people who work in a fill, when we probably make three times what you do, and, hey, you do the same job we do a lot of the time: process trash."

Reeves smiled, pleased with his philosophy. "Anything else, Detective Edo, or am I done?"

"These Mashers seem like self-contained, airtight units. How long before they run out of life support?"

Reeves was getting tired of the questions.

"They can run nonstop for about a week, depending on air use, even have a few compartments with bunks, in case something delays exit, like a tunnel collapse."

"Had any of those lately? Collapses?"

"A minor one, two weeks ago. Nobody injured, just a quick repair job shored it up fine."

"What happened to the surveillance media from that tunnel?"

Reeves looked ahead and didn't answer immediately.

"Surveillance was compromised for about fifteen minutes. Dust and debris filled the tunnels nearby for a while."

"Was surveillance compromised at the dig face where the girl was found?"

"Yes, but it was just a tunnel then. There was no dig face there at that time."

"Why?"

"You just keep pulling those questions out of that hat. We did two core samples off a regular tunnel, by cutting a perpendicular tunnel then a parallel tunnel about forty feet deeper in the fill and sent in the core cutter."

He held up his hand to fend off the next question. "Before you ask, it's a flexible powered tube, about eight feet in diameter, coiled and mounted on the front of a Masher. Retractable saw teeth cover the inside of the tube in rows. The cylinder rotates and extends, cutting into the fill until a sample about twenty feet long is contained in the tubing. We snake it out to the main tunnel and check content to see if it's worth pushing the dig face forward. We fill in behind with castoff material, so the dig room is always about the size it was when you were here last."

"Can a core cutter insert material as well as remove it from a tunnel?"

He gave me a withering look.

"You could, but why? The object is to remove debris, not make more of it. What asshole would do that? Not anyone that works for me, for long. We're at the dig face."

The work had gone on all around the crime scene and had tunneled away behind it. The site itself was untouched, like a free-standing exhibit at a museum with the present passing it by in a rush to the deeper past. It was a grotto with a cavity where the dome had been scooped away, and forlorn beams proclaiming "crime scene" glowed across the front in a grid. Reeves stopped the Masher just feet from the beams and turned to me.

"First and last stop on the tour."

He put the Masher on standby and started to walk to the airlock. I stepped just ahead of him and stood in his way.

"So the tunnel that collapsed led to the core cutter tunnel?"

"All tunnels lead everywhere, like roads. Next question."

"So every tunnel in the entire fill is interconnected?"

Again Reeves didn't answer immediately.

"The northeast entrance is the newer dig, and those tunnels don't connect to us, yet."

"And you're in charge of the northeast operation too?"

He clenched and unclenched his right fist.

"Corzo, the on-site boss, the other one you saw the first time you came, is the one to talk to about the northeast operation. He isn't in today, and, since this site doesn't connect to that site, why bother?"

He moved to walk around me, but I turned back toward the console.

"I've seen what I need to see here, take me to the site of the collapse."

"That area is still unstable."

"You told me it was 'shored up fine.'"

"We don't take chances. You'll have to talk to Corzo, tomorrow maybe."

"You said it was in your section of the fill. Let's go."

He stood still. Something crossed his face, some emotion that looked like anger, but behaved like something else. He went to the console and punched in a code. We turned around slowly and backtracked to the third tunnel on our left. The Masher proceeded into the dark, to stop at a dead end. The supports did look new on either side.

It took four minutes to reach the dead end from the crime scene. We idled there for a moment. Reeves didn't move. We seemed stalled, and it wasn't the Masher. I took a chance.

"So, they told you that no one would come back to ask any questions, that it would just be considered another weird find at the fill. But I bet you wonder, at night, what happened, and why aren't they keeping you informed? You're supposed to be in charge, aren't you? Is it Corzo that changed that?"

Reeves looked at me and blinked. Whatever I saw for a moment was gone.

"You got an extra stop on the tour. Don't say I never gave you anything. Any more questions, you can talk to my lawyer."

I watched as Reeves chose a lighted button on the console for autoguide, and we rode back, through the clean barrier, to the main building in silence. We took off our suits. He finished first and left through the airlock, allowing me time to grab the forgotten comunits from their perch on the wall and slip them in my back pocket. I trailed him toward the office. He looked at me as he passed through the doors and was gone.

Brian was waiting outside the building. In the sunlight, with his freckles, he looked even younger. He was trying to hide that by wearing sunglasses. I got into the pilot seat and we lifted off from the lot before he made any conversation.

"While you were gone, I did a little looking around. I got the license/IDs on all the vehicles in the lot. There's another lot at the northeast side of the fill, maybe we should get the LI-D numbers there, too."

"Good thinking, Brian. You belong in the PUSH Program. You have good instincts."

He beamed.

"Thanks, but I may have been showing off a little, for the girl. Is that an instinct, too?"

I nodded and laughed long.

"Brian, the human race owes its existence to showing off for women. Do you think it worked?"

He passed his photalk from one hand to the other and, as he did, a small square of paper dropped from behind it and fluttered to the foot well. A delectable whiff of scent followed it to the floor. Brian picked it up and tucked it in an inside jacket pocket. He looked straight ahead and smiled again from behind his glasses.

"Got her number."

The northeast lot had a different feeling. As we hovered to land, I looked out past Brian and could see the ocean just east of us. The water and sun took some of the curse off the site.

Still, I landed as far from the fill as the lot allowed. We were in luck. There was a breeze off the Atlantic, so we were upwind and stepped out onto the tarmac into clean air. Without the scent, you could appreciate the size of the endeavor.

From where we stood, the NEAR resembled a huge burial mound. Men in hardhats were moving Mashers, cranes, and bulldozers in and out of large hangars. Several vehicles stood drying in the sun after being pressure-washed. Bulldozers swarmed across the top.

A bully-big worker sauntered toward us as we stepped out of the squadcraft. The too-small webbing inside his hardhat caused it to perch high on his head as if hovering to land. I was sure that he even exercised his scalp muscles. He took off his sunglasses to look us over with tight little eyes. He, like the other outside workers, didn't wear a breather suit. His gloves were tucked in his belt.

"Help you, officers? Is there a problem?"

Everything about him said he was not there to help.

"I'm Detective Edo, this is Officer Shand. There is no problem. We're just asking a few questions about a find in the fill from the other day. It was in the southern dig. We've seen that site, including inside the fill."

"No finds here, just lots and lots of recovery."

He wore a lanyard with an ID dangling from it, but slowly covered the picture with his hand and lifted the card to tuck it into his work-shirt pocket. It didn't matter. I had seen his name and title, and used it.

"Well, George Frye, Site Coordinator, we'd like to look around for a minute in order to understand the day-to-day operations. It seems this side of the fill is the newer one." He said nothing. "Is it the newer part of the fill?"

"Maybe."

"Is there someone here who could show us the operation?"

"I can." He gestured behind him. "There it is."

Brian cleared his throat.

"That's okay. I can call up the entire blueprint, and also the entire history of employment on all the workers here, along with ..."

Frye put up his hand.

"No need. Follow me." He headed toward the entrance, launching into a canned spiel. "We started this dig two years ago, in September. We do mining, but also recovery, maintenance, and auctioning. All the dozers on top of the fill that grade the incoming material are lifted there by the cranes. We have to wash all the equipment in special bays. There they are, the ones that look like hangars. You can see the men sorting the new material over there in that intake area, after it's dropped off. Since you saw the dig face at the other site, you've seen it all. We recover everything, well, almost everything."

Brian asked the obvious.

"What can't be recovered?"

Our guide actually smiled a little square mail-slot smile.

"The moat."

"The moat?"

"It has a more official name, but nobody uses that, and the other names are things like Fuck Hole, Swill, Cum Creek ..."

I stepped on his sentence, "That's enough."

"Anyway, here we are."

He had stopped just short of a huge grate easily the length and width of a Masher. Next to it, a concrete staircase spiraled down into the darkness. Whatever was under the grate sent its smell crawling upward to flow out over the ground into the air. It was a physical assault when it reached us. We actually backed away from it.

Our guide stood his ground and spoke over his shoulder.

"Don't you want to see it?"

Brian looked at me steadily. We had no real reason to take those stairs, except for the fact that the bastard was sure we wouldn't. Brian and I walked past the grate and started down the steps. Frye followed. Vapor lights came on, casting overlapping pools of light as we went down two flights, then they blinked off as we left their area. The odor sank its claws into our clothes.

Brian and I didn't look at each other. We reached a landing that extended into the distance along the side of a body of dark liquid. The light fell on it from above, and streamers of slime hung down from the ironwork of the grate. Brian's stock soared in my estimation when he spoke with an almost normal voice.

"So, what is it?"

"It's the runoff from the trashcraft when they arrive. A hatch opens on the belly of the craft when it hovers over the grate, and whatever is squeezed out of the compressed trash pours into the moat. Sometimes it's gallons, sometimes just a dribble. Whatever it once was, the gel from used diapers, restaurant slops, it ends up in the soup. We have to siphon it off once in a while and bury it. It just doesn't want to be anything else."

As I looked at the fetid stream below us, I flashed on the canyon carving Linda and Carl had "gifted" me. With the passage of time, we humans appeared to be sinking forward. Had "man made this" become "man made this worse"?

Brian and I turned to start back up the stairs but our guide blocked the way. He was not smiling any longer.

"You have wasted my time. You come around without a search warrant, because you don't have any reason to get one, and slow down the routine. Yeah, every time something strange shows up in the other dig, one or two of you show up here. If you want to find something, find your way to the parking lot. Do it soon."

He headed up the steps and didn't look back until he heard me taking the stairs swiftly, two at a time. The sensor lights blinked on suddenly as I passed, as if watching in surprise. I was waiting at the top blocking his path this time. I used a conversational tone.

"What if I told you that what we found at the south site came from this site?"

"I would tell you to get a new day job. The two sites aren't connected. The tunnels don't connect."

"They did, briefly. There was a collapse, but it was actually right where the sites connect, and something was moved into the south site. It was big. It would have needed to be transported by a Masher. We'd like to see all the surveillance from the last two weeks, from just before the collapse."

"If only you had asked sooner. We just don't keep our surveillance data that long. 'One Day, Overlay.' That's our motto. Sorry."

Brian had caught up to us. He had taken a few photalk shots of the moat, so he arrived just in time to hear most of Frye's words.

"'One day, Overlay?' You're required by law to keep records longer than that. We could stop all operations until we are satisfied in court that you have changed that policy. It can take a while to get that hearing."

Frye's look could have pushed Brian down the stairwell. He started to speak, then thought better of it, then did speak.

"I know it takes you a few days to put a stop on what we do. So go do it. Whatever you thought you could see, you can't, no proof exists. We've got deep enough pockets to be back in business before you get your next donut."

With that, Frye strode away toward the work vehicles. Brian turned to me, the question all over him.

"What's a donut?"

At least some urban myths do die.

Brian and I went to stand by the squadcraft for a few minutes, letting the breeze drive the smell out of our clothes, although I knew I would throw mine away that night. It was ironic that they would probably end up near where we were standing.

I got in the driver's side and suggested we exit slowly over the employee flight lot to take quick shots of the vehicles and do just what Brian had threatened: check out the employees and try for a work stop order.

Brian pulled out the briefkit and stretched the silicone screen from "hand size" to "share size" and got panoramic views of the cars. We could have checked the license numbers while en route, but there were many, and we were not where we had told dispatch we would be, so I asked Brian to wait until we reached our next destination. He nodded, but looked puzzled, so I asked what the problem was.

"I was just thinking about what happened back there, with Frye. At the academy, we got to carry briefkits along with our photalks into the field, so we could check all kinds of background information right at the scene. I don't understand why we only have photalks to carry with us and can only access other information from the squadcraft itself."

"You know, I asked my first partner, Carl, the same question. He said the department had discovered that officers who carried briefkits got lost in the overload of information when they carried them to the scene. It was like sailing by using an onboard monitor, when you only had to look up to see what the wind was doing. The department decided that massive information was a good tool at the academy, but in practice, where the first look at a crime scene is crucial and time is critical, officers should rely most on their training and instincts, and check the wind, so to speak. The information is always there in the squadcraft or at the precinct. The crime scene isn't."

Brain looked disappointed, but nodded reluctantly. I could see he wasn't convinced. We continued toward the Library of Records, LiBrec. Brian stayed quiet for most of the ride, but spoke up just before landing.

"It's too bad that Frye knew what he was talking about with the court. They probably can get right back to work. Also, without the surveillance, hey, why are you smiling?"

"Brian, we don't need it. All their workers have comunits, Reeves told me. All comunits have G dots. We can do a comunit check to see where everyone was at any given time. We only have to prove a single unit moved from one tunnel system to another. We might get a group of units. Either way, it supports my theory that something big was moved from site to site."

"What? What was moved?"

"Brian, there is a reason I'm not going to tell you, and it's a good reason. When all is said and done, I will tell you. Let's just hope that the G dot tracking doesn't occur to Frye before we can get the information. We will have to get some clearances for that."

We hurried into LiBrec to pick up the documents for the rape kits and returned to the precinct by eleven. Brian actually seemed to want to do paperwork, not like the Dieter Freak, but to help me.

He asked if he could check the Li-D's and the NEAR owner list before the other new reports that had magically appeared during our absence. I told him he was the boss and that I had to follow up on an informant. I left him peering into the holoscreen, pushing data around with his long fingers, lost in the facts.

I accessed the G dot location on Sniff. I had casually attached one to the underside of the strutstep on his vehicle during my visit. It was only a half inch in diameter so it would go unnoticed unless someone knew to look for it.

The coordinates were odd. He was parked on the outskirts of a Rim City mall. I reached the location in fifteen minutes to find his cobblecraft isolated in a corner of the lot. Not shopping, apparently. I lighted on the asphalt behind his craft. It felt wrong in every way. I drew my magnum, held it up and ready, and approached the driver's side.

Sniff was there, and alive, barely. Even through the door I could hear his tortured breathing. His eyes were closed, his head thrown back as if he were drowning in the air. Sputum trailed down his chin and shirt front. No blood was visible.

I called for an ambulance on my own photalk, not wanting to use the police Cyphersafe line. I didn't want to explain to anyone why I was there, yet. There was an ambulance craft in the area, so they arrived in less than a minute. I didn't know the crew, different district.

The first paramedic took one look through the craft window and backtracked two feet. He went to the ambulance and donned a breather pack along with his partner.

"Better stand back and upwind, detective, no point in taking any chances, right?"

They shoveled Sniff out of the front seat and onto a hyperhelium raft to float him to the ambulance. I followed them to Rim City Memorial. They hurried him into an isolation unit. Check-in was quick, as I told them I was only supposed to meet this man for an informal talk to see if he knew something about a case I was handling.

No one seemed interested in the patient, partly because the human ruin on the raft did not invite curiosity, and neither did I. They were only very interested in the fact that I was willing to pay for his care.

I waited in the hall outside the isolation unit. It wasn't long before a tall doctor in blue scrubs came up the hall and looked at me before entering the anteroom. He had such calm eyes, large and clear, that took in everything, accepted everything, and seemed able to fix everything just by gazing. He didn't need a bedside manner; his eyes did the work for him. A fawning resident followed him, even imitated his walk.

They came out in fifteen minutes, the tall one leading. I had watched them take off gloves and rebreathers in the anteroom before reentering the hallway.

The tall doctor approached me and his gaze fell on me like a blessing.

"I am Doctor Augustini. You called the ambulance for this patient? Is he a relative?"

"No, he is an informant for our precinct. I found him in his craft and thought he needed medical attention."

"I wish I could say your quick thinking saved his life, Officer …?"

"Edo. Detective Edo. So, has he …?"

"No, not yet, but it is a certainty. Do you have any idea how long he has been ill?"

"I met with him just two days ago, and he seemed fine."

"You spoke to this man forty-eight hours ago? That would seem impossible. No pneumonia moves that quickly. They used to call rapid failure of the lungs and organs 'galloping pneumonia,' but this would be a new record, a 'flash-failure.' Perhaps it is not even pneumonia, although it presents that way. It could be ingested, inhaled, spread by touch, or even invade the body through a cut or abrasion."

I was intrigued at this point as the doctor explained, "In the event that it is contagious, and I would err on the side of caution, you need to be treated with wide-spectrum antibiotics and antivirals, perhaps also gamma globulin, even before we can determine whatever this is.

It may be that virulent, although, if he was well two days ago and is now dying, you would likely be very ill by now through contact with him,"

I wasn't sure what to do next, but felt the good doctor would know best.

He said, "Let us just take the precaution. I will arrange for the injections, yes, sorry, actual injections. You will not like them, and you will not like me for six hours or so. The medications are very powerful. It will be better than dying, however. You can refuse…"

"Dr. Augustini, I have a feeling no one refuses your advice."

His eyes virtually patted my head.

"Thank you for your confidence, Detective, I'm sure I would take your recommendation on a police matter."

"Speaking of police matters, Dr. Augustini, did he say anything at all? Sorry, but I needed his input on a case, and I was hoping he had some information for me."

"I believe he said something to my resident while I was looking at his chart. He could have been delirious, so I am not sure he said anything useful. There is no point in exposing yourself to him further. He is in a coma. That is likely the kindest thing that can befall him now. Let me go order your medications. The nurse will be here in a moment to take care of you," he said as he turned to his colleague.

"Dr. Jarvis, did you hear the patient say something? Detective Edo is asking. I'm sorry, but I must go. We will contact you regarding the patient."

Dr. Jarvis and I watched him move off to cast his spell on others. I turned to the shadowy resident, who had the opposite effect on the viewer as his mentor. He wore thick glasses, almost unheard of in a world of easy laser correction. His vision had to be truly terrible to be beyond the scope of surgery.

"Dr. Jarvis, did you hear my informant say something?" He pushed his glasses back up on his nose.

"Yes, he was repeating something. I could barely hear him, but he kept saying, 'Inside outside, inside outside.' Oh, he also said, 'Outside inside.' That made it so much clearer." He smirked at his own wit.

My expression stopped him. He looked down like a chastised child and practically kicked the tile with his toe. "Well, that is what he said. Then he just lapsed into unconsciousness."

Jarvis's glasses had slipped again, so he tilted his head up and corrected them, then gave me a narrow look, "Enjoy your shots."

With that little stab of retaliation, Dr. Augustini's doppelgänger hustled after his god.

Inside outside. The words seemed to mean nothing, but they were important enough to Sniff to be his last.

15

Dr. Augustini did not lie. How could he?

The nurse warned that the first two hours were the worst after the injections, as the medications targeted your specific epigenetic markers and put you through a condensed hell of side effects.

I could barely get out of the squadcraft at the precinct and had sweat through my shirt, so I dragged myself to the lockers where I kept a spare. My private phone chirped. A robotic voice identified itself as the RimCity Memorial message system. The patient, Number 12-745, brought in by Edo, K., had died, and had been moved to the morgue. I was to call to make arrangements for his "placement."

Also, I was patched to a message from Dr. Augustini. He had called to let me know that tests on Sniff indicated the illness was not contagious, and, in fact, the biological agent had died with Sniff. He was satisfied that I was out of danger, but he was going to do more research on the contagion. He apologized for any discomfort the injections had caused but suggested that they would serve me against future colds and flulike diseases: great news, a little late.

I shrugged into a new long-sleeved shirt, but fresh clothes did not make me feel any better. I sat down wearily on the bench between the rows of lockers. I had not let myself think about Sniff until now. I didn't even know his real name. As Augustini had said, it seemed impossible that he could become so ill in forty-eight hours.

Actually, it had been only twenty-four hours since he had gone to the fill sale just last night. Maybe he hadn't gone, and this was something else. No, he had gone there with the prospect of all those credits for his time. It had to do with the fill somehow. Had something happened to him "inside," or did he learn something "inside?" Did someone connect him to me and leave him for me as another message?

No, they wouldn't have taken a chance on his being able to actually tell me anything. He was deliberately left to die a sudden but agonizing death alone. I was sweating again, but not because of the meds. I had brought Sniff to his last breath, for two hundred credits.

I sat alone in the locker bay for fifteen minutes, trying to decide how to proceed. On my way back to the precinct, I had arranged for Sniff's cobblecraft to be sealed and moved to a private lot, to keep it out of impound.

The precinct had to be tainted; I felt it. Help was not around me in this building. I felt terrible, in every way. I bowed my head in my hands. Suddenly, shoes appeared in my line of vision. I stood up like a shot and almost knocked Brian into a locker. He looked at me with his head cocked to one side, so much like Clyde that I laughed feebly. The expressions moved across his face at comic speed, from surprise to puzzlement to concern.

"Are you okay? You look terrible. I saw the squadcraft out there, but you didn't come up to the Cave, so I came looking. This little box arrived for you by courier. I thought it might be important. I got it scanned and questioned the delivery guy. He had a legitimate ID and vehicle; I checked it all out with the company." He held out the four-inch-square box, with security scan okays light-stamped on every side.

"Thanks, Brian, sorry, you just caught me at a bad moment. I'll explain later."

"I hope you don't mind, but I looked at the scan. It's an old key, and a slip of paper, that's all. Hey, I was doing my real job too. Two rape kits finished. I decided I would do those first after all, before researching the Li-D's from the fill."

He looked at the box in my hands. He wore his curiosity like his badge, right up front, but he was too polite to pry. "Well, I'm going to work on those licenses and the NEAR owner names, but if you need any help with anything, let me know."

I saluted him and he laughed as he left the locker bay. I turned the box over in my hands. No return address. No handwriting. A printed label with an incomplete address showing only Detective K. Edo, Precinct 110, NYCI Police Department.

The box gave off faint metallic tics of sound when shaken. The tape peeled off easily from the top seam. The key and paper were in a sealed plastic bag inside a larger bag. I could tell the key was a copy with its generic top and three triangular holes. It was very old-fashioned, as nearly everything was keyless now.

I didn't open the bag, but unfurled it from inside the box by the corner and turned it to see what was written on the paper above the key. A number, faded and faint, as if written long ago: *1345*. There was nothing else on the paper.

Safety deposit box? Those didn't have keys any longer. The year 1345 was during the Middle Ages, Black Plague era. Something to do with the sickness? Nothing else came to mind that had any significance. A football score, 13–45. I wished I were in command of my faculties and not still reeling from the medications. This would be going better for me if I were … better.

I looked at the paper again. It was a kind of blue-gray, and in the top lefthand corner was … .what was that? A watermark? It looked like a dent in the paper. I brought the bag so close to my face that my breath misted the surface for a moment. I held it up to the light. Watermark. A small dented circle. 1345 Circle, Circle Drive or Street? There were smaller circles in part of the watermark, was it a half moon? 1345 Half Moon? 1345 Crescent Moon? Nothing, no bells, no recognition. 1345 Luna, Lune, loon, moon.

I looked at it again. The circle was a shade lighter than the paper, the whole circle. Full moon? Blue-gray paper. Blue moon. It was the next street over from my parent's house. Was there a 1345 Blue Moon? It had another meaning too.

It was good that I was not expected anywhere for a while. I signed out at a terminal in the locker room and left the building through the side exit. By taking a commuter train and getting on and off at least twice at each stop, then renting a craft near one of the stops, I felt I had thrown off any followers.

I stepped into Hardware World, which was so large they had maps of the layout at each entrance. I didn't have that kind of time. I laid the bag down on the nearest information counter in front of a female attendant reading a vieunit. She continued staring at her screen, even after I spoke.

"Can you scan this key and make a copy without taking it out of the bag?"

Her gaze shifted directly to the bag as she blew her bangs out of her eyes with a condescending breath.

"You're in luck. We've only been able to do that for most of this century." She finally looked up at me and her eyes changed along with her attitude. "Well, of course we can. Umm, sorry, I was in the middle of something." She drew her hand through her long brown hair and tossed her head.

"Let me take you to the QuicKey unit."

She was enjoying having me follow her as she swayed her way to the machine, which stood what seemed to be a quarter mile from her desk. She placed the bag between two light boxes and pressed a green button. A blue LED light poured over the key from above and below and clicked off just as the duplicate slid down a chute into a catch bin. Joy, as her name badge identified her, lifted the golden replica and placed it in my hand and curled my fingers around it with hers.

"Here it is, it's on the house, just for you. I'll do a QuicKey for you any time, gorgeous."

If I hadn't been well-medicated and in a hurry, I would possibly have laughed out loud, or arrested her, I'm not sure which. As it was, I just half-smiled, picked up the original from the light box, and headed to the cashier.

16

The little house on Blue Moon was like its street name, pale in the late morning. The grass put its fingers out tentatively over the edges of the front walk. The hedges bordering the lawn flirted with perfection but missed. Someone cared for the place, just not for the past week or so. I clicked the safety off my magnum as I walked to the front porch. My reflection came to meet me in the mirror-finish red lacquer door. Floor-to-ceiling pocket windows on either side revealed slices of a long hallway to a room loaded with sun.

The replikey kissed the inside of the lock, and a slight push swung the door inward until it slowed and stopped. My magnum was up and ready.

No furniture, no pictures, blond wood floors. The quiet felt like the only thing that lived there. Five steps, ten, staying close to the right wall. The hall became the kitchen, full of light and nothing else, except a handwritten note on the counter, held down by a cobalt blue paperweight shaped like a breaking wave. I knew the handwriting. The lilting text was unmistakable.

Darling Kirt:

Do you remember? You must, or you wouldn't be here. This was the best way we could think of to let you know we are safe. If you knew what the riddle meant, you also know where we are, or rather, where we have left word for you.

Your father got us to safety. Do you remember when he remodeled the greenhouse after Jack disappeared? He was doing much more than that. He knew they were watching our house, but who would be watching this little house on Blue Moon? No one. So he bought it and built a tunnel from the greenhouse to the basement here. No one suspected with all that construction and digging and dirt.

We have had everything ready for a long time. When you are ready, you can follow. There's a new Ninex in the side port of this house. Use it to come to us.

All our Love, darling,

I exhaled. My mother's note was legitimate. She never signed her letters, saying that it was too much like goodbye, which she hated. If she had been coerced, she would have signed it, which would seem right but would be a warning to anyone who knew her. I looked into the glassy depths of the paperweight and remembered the Blue Moon.

Jack really caused the whole thing to happen. He came home from classes the day before spring break of his senior year in high school to tell us he had been invited to the Lake Tahoe vacation home of a school friend and was leaving within hours.

I was stunned. It seemed a betrayal to us all, especially to me. My parents had planned a surprise family trip, but Jack was oblivious to that and began throwing things in a travel pack immediately. My parents looked at each other and sighed. He was headstrong and charming and, most of all, eighteen—things that combined to get him his way in nearly everything. He actually ruffled my hair before hurtling out the door, snow skis over one shoulder.

Youth and prolonged anger are a strange combination in a thirteen-year-old, but I couldn't shrug it off. The remains of our family prepared to go on the surprise trip without Jack. I coiled like a pit viper in my room until we left the next morning.

I stared at my thin long arms crossed in front of me and refused to look out the transport window as we passed over the FAR, the Federal Agricultural Regions, heading toward the West Coast. We landed at LAX and picked up a shining new rental cruiser. We headed north along the coast for a short distance until a clutch of buildings appeared below that drew my father down to the lot in their midst.

I couldn't help looking around when we landed. Curiosity reverses the tidal pull of many emotions.

The Blue Moon Resort anchored itself haphazardly to the edge of California, almost as much a part of the Pacific as of the coast. Our rooms all faced the sea, and the cliff face fell away directly below the windows. A narrow beach peeked out shyly when the tide backed down, the sand dotted with rock outcroppings. We stood at the windows in a row, silent in the face of all that blue rippling to the horizon. I turned to my parents, puzzled.

"How did you pick this place? It's great but is it famous or something, or famous for something?"

They laughed, and looked into each other's eyes. My mother even blushed.

"We came here on our honeymoon after friends recommended it. Other people owned it then, but it is still so much like it was, thank goodness. It is even the reason we live where we live at home. We had such a wonderful time here that we were attracted to our neighborhood by the street named Blue Moon."

I was immersed in the story as my mother continued, "The house for sale there was not what we wanted, but we found just the right house on the next street, so we felt it was meant to be. We always wanted to bring you and Jonathan here, but evidently bringing just you here is what was meant to be: Providence at work from beginning to end."

She stepped a little closer to me and I noticed for the first time that I was taller than my mother. She leaned her head against my shoulder for a moment. "I hope you like it here, darling. There is much to do, and so little time!"

I wondered then why she turned away quickly, touched her eyes, tossed her hair, and smiled. I thought she meant we only had a week's vacation. It took some time for me to realize her tears were not about length, but height.

My room boasted all the same tones as the sea and land. I pulled the bed to the plate-glass wall. Possibly, this was going to be … not bad, I told myself, healing reluctantly.

We dined at the restaurant that night, thinking we would try other places over the coming days. It was completely dark when we arrived at the door and entered. Mica glass lanterns lit the hall to the main dining room.

A powerfully built blond woman blazed up quietly out of the half-light to lead us to the open deck. Teak walls, teak tables, and carved chairs gleamed in the moonlight. A team of equally powerful blond waiters and sommeliers moved through the restaurant, filling glasses, flourishing skewers and steaming plates, and refilling glasses. We learned they were all one family. They behaved like the schools of fish in the depths nearby, and somewhere in the kitchen was another of their school, using the bounty drawn from those depths to feed us.

Always, under the soft murmur of conversation and silverware clicking, there was the sea. I can still hear its sound: Shurrrrrrrrr … shurrrrrr … Fading each time like a voice before sleep. Occasionally there was a break in the rhythm, and we would all look up, waiting for the sea to finish her sentence.

We took diving lessons the following days and saw brilliant golden orange Garibaldi fish, round as plates, nipping at the underwater formations near La Jolla Cove. That time granted me the love and skill for diving, which made the oil rig job possible five years later.

We visited Santa Monica Pier and I tried surfing off Point Loma near San Diego. We went inland and walked among the giants in Sequoia National Forest. We cruised above the spiraling road to Mount Palomar and marveled at the photo gallery on the wall showing pinwheel galaxies and star nurseries. That week also showed me a world I could populate with my own dreams, separate from my family, from Jack.

The owners of Blue Moon became our friends, and we remained in touch. We dined with them—and the sea— every night.

When we returned home and reunited with Jack, he filled the room with his stories of skiing and climbing, and bonfires at midnight by the lake. I smiled and kept my adventures to myself. In fact, Jack never really asked us many questions about our trip. He probably thought few places could compare with Tahoe. I knew better.

In his thoughtless way, Jack broke the tether between us. It did much for me yet stayed with me, as many painful things do. Even standing in the empty kitchen of this strange house, I felt it all again.

I walked to the side port door and opened it to see the Ninex, as promised. I went into the basement to find the locked door leading toward my parents' home. I was tempted to unlock it and travel to our house, but someone might still be watching, since it had only been a day or two since my parents' escape.

Before leaving, I reached to collect the letter and paperweight from the counter, and then stopped. They were safer here than with me and would mean nothing to others even if discovered.

For a moment, the prospect of flying off toward California was so clean and inviting. I was tempted to show up at Five Points, pick up Suli, and leave the evidence for someone else to decipher. Why stay? Jack was dead, somewhere in the NEAR, and someone was enjoying knowing I knew it. Sniff was dead. Claire was dead. I could say I was too close to the case. I should and could just drop it all on Brian Shand and the department and ... those thoughts lasted about ten seconds.

No. Someone had to pay for Jack and all the others. I would collect on that debt. I closed the door slowly on 1345 Blue Moon to return to work. Suli and work were the only worlds I had now.

Brian was almost vibrating with news when I clocked back in at the Cave.

"Weird stuff is happening. You know the list of names you gave me to match against NEAR ownership? Well, the NEAR is owned by no less than seven holding companies, and no names matched the directors, or even employees, of those companies.

So I looked at the companies that hold *those* companies, and there are fifteen of them. All are utilities or infrastructure firms, all global too. Yeah, they're the suits who allow people to get places, buy things, and have water to drink."

"Sounds as if somebody has control issues," I said.

Brian chuckled.

"Guess they have Grid Greed."

"Let's expose them. You don't need a shower or food for the rest of your life, do you?" I asked him.

"Thanks, I'll stick with the battle I've got, trying to find names that match your list. I did find one. Whoever really owns the NEAR is layers and layers into the background."

"Who was the match?'

"Levitt."

I honed in on his eyes when Brian spoke the name. He hurried to say, "Levitt *was* an owner name, but hasn't been for about a year, and the only sub-text, Levitt, Claire, was an eye-opener. That record and anything associated in any social or secure site had been picked down to a skeleton entry by some carrion-eating hacker: not even a picture remains, just last, first."

He was so into his findings, Brian didn't note my whispered profanity and continued his report.

"Remember the Li-D's I was going to check? Something really strange there too, not with the ones where we first landed, but with the plates from the northeast lot where we talked with Muscle Head. About 70 percent of the vehicles are registered to parolees, mostly B and E's, craft theft, strong-arm stuff. Not one of them has been in trouble for at least four years. Maybe the management wants to give some of society a second chance."

"Or maybe management wants a pool of very special talents."

Brian looked puzzled. He stroked his chin and talked to himself.

"For what? Maybe they use them like the railroads used to use street types for security, 'bulls', to keep people out of the rail yards. But who would want to break into a dump?" He laughed at his own question.

Yes, who?

I steered him away from the landfill investigation and helped him finish two more piles of paperwork. We got some lunch at a local dive. I was beginning to feel almost human. I called Suli from the lot while Brian paid the bill, as he insisted he would.

Suli's face on my photalk screen brought back hot memories of that morning. Her voice moved me as always, but in many different ways now. I mentioned Brian, and his help, but that I missed her. We agreed I would stop by for her at about eight that evening. I had to go home first to shower and feed Clyde before going to Suli's. I wanted her near me, wanted to kiss that bruise, and much more. When Brian emerged from the restaurant, I motioned him over to stand next to me so we would both be visible to Suli. I did the introductions.

"Suli Masters, this is Brian Shand. He's been my associate today, and he's a Tech Beast. Brian, Suli is my usual partner, one of the best detectives in the city."

Brian colored slightly and said, "I'm a poor substitute I'm sure, Ms. Masters."

Suli looked truly puzzled.

"Strange, Kirt has had nothing but praise for you. Are there two Brian Shands?" Smiles all around.

"I look forward to meeting you in person," she said.

We spoke for a few moments in a three-cornered conversation, moderated by Suli, and said our goodbyes. Almost before the photalk screen went blank, Brian exhaled and said, "Wow, she is wow. Do you think she always had that voice? There's some kind of subliminal purr in there, plus maybe a sort of … smokiness or something …" His sentence trailed off as he tried to categorize his impression. He had hit it perfectly.

"Wish I'd said that," was all I could add.

Brian and I finished out the day by clearing my work station of papers. He actually grinned when we reached the worn top, its raw metal showing in places from years of abuse. With the point of my scissors, he carved a circle in the finish, and scratched "Brian was here" in the center. I tried to look serious; didn't work. I just couldn't resist smiling.

"That is destruction of city property."

"Don't worry," Brian said, "by tomorrow it will be buried forever under a mountain of new reports." He pretended to punch my shoulder playfully.

"Thanks, I needed that reminder."

We parted company in the lot. He shook my hand.

"Today was great, Detec— Kirt. I hope they assign me to you tomorrow."

"I do too. You were invaluable, Brian, and you might even get a date out of this day's work."

His faced lit up and he said, "Yeah! How long do I wait to call her? Are there rules? There should be rules, a rule book, dating laws. Oh, on second thought, that would be bad. Men would never live it down. Well, see you soon, I think."

"Brain, tell you what. Just show up here tomorrow morning. I want to find a way to get you assigned to us."

There was barely room on his face for that smile of his. He walked backward a few steps and saluted just as I had saluted him in the locker bay, then turned and jogged toward twilight.

I landed on my shadowed rooftop just after dark. The spring air stood still, stunned by the speed of the sunset. I had stopped to buy a plant for Suli, some sort of evergreen. The scent took over the interior of the craft.

I breathed it in deeply and imagined the forest. I would move its effect into my place, along with Suli, this night.

Clyde's shadow coursed the length of the apartment through the frosted glass. As I turned to make sure my vehicle recessed into its bay, a smashing blow from behind drove me to my knees. Before I could even move, a searing pain ran from my shoulder to my head, like fire up a ridge. My field of vision narrowed to a dot—and winked out.

17

The floor was moving. The vibration and a slight sliding sensation told me I was on my way somewhere. My head throbbed.

I was lying on my back looking up at a white ceiling with rows of recessed lights, lots of them, nearly covering the ceiling's surface. They were not all in use. Just a few shone into my eyes. Operating room? No, I wouldn't be lying on the floor, hopefully. It hurt, but I rolled my head slowly to one side. No windows.

The space looked familiar. Airlock. Masher. I felt something odd around my neck. I reached up to feel a metal torque—cool to the touch, with a graduated closure at the back. It was a necktite. We used them at the precinct to subdue otherwise uncontrollable suspects. Human rights groups had a standing complaint against their use, but they were no more or less humane than Tasers, Hotspray, or stun bots, all of which had varied strength levels.

An officer could use a remote to control the tightening of the collar and also give a mild to potent electric shock, until the suspect either cooperated or was rendered unconscious. The device could also be auto-set to give graduated punishment to the wearer, depending on how close he or she got to the officer.

Every member of the force who had the right to use a necktite had had one used on him, or her, so I knew what could be done to me. I didn't know which setting was in use. There was only one way to find out. Still trying to clear my head, I closed my eyes. I opened them to see a figure blocking the light.

"You talk in your sleep."

I couldn't see my own face, but if it betrayed half my shock, it should have been enough to stun Jack, the brother I had mourned until that moment. He loomed over me in a breather suit with gloves in one hand and the necktite remote in the other. He had changed little in seven years, except for his eyes. They used to have a light in them. It had been replaced by a simmering glow, like the dead end of a fire.

"What? No 'Welcome back, Jack'? Okay, a bad way to reunite, but it was the only way, believe me."

I could not speak. There was no one word for the clot of emotion caught in my throat. Was it rage or hate, long-held tension, destroyed faith? I just looked at him. He stepped back a bit to look down at me. I sat up slowly.

Jack smiled. I winced as the necktite constricted ever so slightly when he pressed the control to test it.

"Sorry," he said, "but I really prefer the silent treatment. Let me answer all the likely questions without interruption. I disappeared of my own free will, detective, got an offer that was too good to refuse. It is hard, hard to turn down four million credits, all the women you can eat, unlimited travel, well, with a dye job and moustache. Only drawback is the moustache. Itchy."

He had removed any last hope that he was somehow not a part of all this. I had to recover myself, when what I wanted to do was kill my own brother with my hands. He relaxed the necktite to let me know it was my turn to speak. I only needed one word.

"Why?"

"Oh, you wouldn't like what I've had to do, but then, we all have to do something, don't we? Look at us. Seven years ago you were diving on oil rigs instead of going to school. I was working with Dad, going to be a captain of industry in a marble building with a big office. I kept thinking about our little talk at our parents' house, remember? I suddenly realized how right you were," he sneered.

"I wanted to be you," Jack accused, "away, free, doing whatever the hell I wanted. But everything was on me, the eldest, the schmuck in the suit. Twenty-three and I thought I was dead already. Then this thing happens. I'm in the parking structure and the most beautiful woman, inhumanly beautiful woman, slows down next to me in her Ninex hovercraft and says, 'Come with me if you want to live,' and laughs. I actually flicked off my shoe for good effect, dropped my briefkit and photalk on the pavement, and got in. I still see her on occasion, but she was just sent to make the offer."

I think he had forgotten I was there. He probably hadn't had anyone to tell his story to, ever. He went on in a disconnected voice, his eyes blank, recounting the moment.

"And go with her I did. They threatened to kill all of you, my family, if I ever tried to escape, but they sensed I had escaped *to* them. It was perfect. You were all safe, I was free, rich, and just had to do a job for them now and then."

It didn't make sense. I had recovered my voice. I had to know more.

I asked, "You were already rich, you could have had all the money and women you wanted. Dad would have understood if you needed to look around and get away."

"Oh, he would have understood for a year, maybe two. Then it would have been the slow guilt trip to hell, my not wanting to sell bio-techs, or not wanting to be a lawyer or a doctor, something suitable, befitting my station."

He said it with his head tilted up as if he smelled something. He walked around me, eyeing me like a specimen on a pin.

"Even you had to do something. Do you like your job, little brother, looking under society's rocks for insects, picking up the same insect for the ninth or tenth time, hoping you don't have to pick him up again the next day? Or maybe you only handle the serious crimes now. I follow your life when I can. You are newsworthy, Kirt. Do you like it?"

This person was as strange to me as any of the broken, drugged, psychotic, wealthy, or hell-hole people I had ever questioned who eventually couldn't wait to tell me why they did what they did. So my "gift" had been right. Jack was dead, to me, to us. I had to keep him talking. He was going to give me something useful if I could keep the focus on him.

"This isn't about me, it's about you. It's all about you. Do you know you nearly destroyed our parents? You selfish son of a bitch, you wanted a life without responsibility, never mind what it cost everyone else."

Jack responded, "I thought about that, but there really wasn't anything I could do. Once I got in that Ninex, there was no reversal. Anyway, our parents had you, and look at the result: a hero. I made room for you to be the hero instead of me. You practically owe me."

He was feeling good. Now was my chance.

"So your job is to kidnap, maybe kill people, maybe the girl we just found. Claire, wasn't that her name?"

No flicker of reaction from him.

"Oh, you didn't find her. We brought her to you, so that you would come to us."

"Who is 'we'?" I asked.

Jack smiled, "Let me show you something."

He gestured toward the airlock with the necktite remote. I got up slowly. He gave me a moment to brush myself off and straighten my clothes. I walked ahead of him. He pointed to a breather suit. He kept the remote trained on me as I got into it. I struggled a little with the suit and helmet. He picked up a laser magnum from the console and clipped it to a magnetic port on his suit's belt.

When I was ready, he closed the inner door and punched the airlock release. We stepped out into the tunnel, identical to all the tunnels with its chemlights every fifty feet or so. We trudged carefully in the direction of a white wall blocking the entire tunnel from floor to ceiling. We took stairs up one side of what appeared to be a loading dock. Several bays stood empty where large vehicles could pull up to roller doors with fitted accordion mechanisms that would create a seal between the vehicles and the bay.

Jack gestured across the cement expanse to a door at one end. We stepped into another airlock and a blast of ultraviolight along with a powerful wind shear completely cleaned the chamber and replaced the fetid air that had followed us inside.

He gestured for me to get out of the suit. I fumbled with it a little and finally shed the whole thing. He again gestured and I hung the suit on a wall hook. He pushed a button on the necktite remote, which sharply constricted until I stepped farther away from him.

He expertly removed his suit and gathered the remote and gun in seconds. Jack wore a black knit shirt and charcoal slacks: No wonder he had blended so well with the shadows on the penthouse roof. He rippled with muscles that had nothing to do with youth or joy and all to do with repetition.

We stepped into a hallway that could have been in any building. We could have been colleagues, going for a drink after work, except for the weapons. He walked behind me, the lasermagnum trained on the small of my back, telling me to turn left or right in a seemingly endless labyrinth of halls, all identical except for a small sign at each intersection.

Each sign had an "A" as the letter, then a symbol. I had never seen anything like the symbols. The "A" was the only constant, so I hoped it meant it was a main route, or section. We saw no one for several minutes, but finally. at the end of a corridor, we stopped at a door like all the others we had passed. Jack told me to open it.

"You open it," I countered.

"Don't you want to know why you are here? It's behind that door."

Neither of us moved. Jack just looked at me steadily, his gun pointed at my face. He seemed willing to stand there until the stars went dark. I opened the door.

18

When you think you are about to die, your senses go into overdrive. You hear the molecules touching your eardrums; the air has a taste. Your pupils turn black and deep and huge, to take in the last moments of light. I did not die, but my senses staggered.

I looked out into a huge space, open perhaps a mile into the deep distance. The "sky" curved over us in a small version of the real thing. The artificial illumination was so much like the sun I was disoriented. Trees stood at the edge of a long blue lake with that incredible light sparkling on its surface, but we were in an impossibly large atrium with balconies along several stories, all of it buried in a landfill.

Inside, outside. Sniff's best attempt to tell me now made sense. How he got this far, I would never know, but he must have seen this. I hoped so. Walkways dappled with "sun" meandered under the trees, going off in several directions into the "forest." Jack directed me onto a path to the left, toward the lake. Birds fluttered in the branches or drank at the water's edge. I looked up for the light source, but it appeared to be the sky itself that glowed. Jack's voice came from behind me.

"Think of it as a giant nightlight, or daylight. We can make the sky any color we want: It can be sunset, night, we have the constellations."

We stopped next to a clearing. Rustic Adirondack chairs dotted the nearby lakeshore. Jack said to walk out onto the grass and choose a seat. I took the chair at the end, which gave me full view of all the others. Jack sat in the next chair down, gun ready, and smiled.

"Always the cop, aren't you, covering the flank."

"What is … this?"

"It's the future, actually. We think that when the air quality gets too terrible for life, or there is the inevitable nuclear event, we might have the perfect retreat. It's totally self-contained. Because landfills have to protect and also control the aquifers beneath them, we have our own water, and air, supplied through filtered horizontal drill paths, hydroponics farms, food storage all along those corridors, fuel for the generators, and God knows we know what to do with the garbage."

Jack laughed. I remembered how I had wished I could hear that laugh just once more. Hell, it's true. Be careful what you wish for.

"Why are we here?"

Jack shook his head. He wore a rueful smile.

"Surrounded by one of the most incredible environments on Earth, and you are focused on the facts. You will have your answers soon enough. Now is your chance to just appreciate this. You are meeting the one responsible for all of it. He wants to meet with you alone, right here."

Immediately, as if on cue, a silent vehicle approached out of the trees and stopped near us. It was a small suspended craft, hovering just above the path. The rear passenger door slid into itself and a figure stepped out onto the ground.

In a lifetime, you must interact with a lot of people. Most you don't remember. You would not forget meeting this one, even if you willed it. He was easily six feet tall and slender. He walked looking straight ahead, not down at his feet. Everything about him was straight, from his dark hair to his tie to his stride. The sharp perfection of his gray suit cut the eye.

We would have a private audience. *Why? Why me?* He had gone to great lengths for this moment.

From my life I knew that the best criminals are always working a deal, and they trust no one. We stood up to meet the visitor. I swayed slightly and stumbled into Jack for a moment. He pushed me off, his gun still trained on me.

"After-effects of your knockout drug," I said softly.

Jack stood beside me but focused on his approaching superior.

"Sir, this is my brother, Detective Kirtland Edo, delivered as promised."

Jack's hero leaned slightly toward him as if to touch his arm, but he did not. Jack turned with a look at me, and then left us. I stood in front of Jack's chair. The man went behind what had been my chair, tipped it up from the backrest, and brought it to face mine, with his back to the lake. He was staging this for me, so I would get the full impact of his person with his great creation as the setting. I had counted on it.

"Please sit down, Detective Edo. I saw you sway momentarily. I hope you have recovered from our 'twilight sleep.' It's a precaution really, for your protection as well as ours. I am John Cromwell."

The name Cromwell was instantly familiar, and his face meant something to me, but I was not sure why. I felt the answer forming just outside my memory. It would come to me. I waited, and didn't speak. He settled into his own chair as I sat in mine. I leaned forward slightly, not able to be comfortable.

"Welcome to NEAR Earth."

"Interesting welcome when you have to render your visitors unconscious and bring them at gunpoint."

"As I said, it is a precaution. I hope you will let me explain."

"Do I have a choice?"

He tilted his head slightly to the left, and smiled. He paused and drew a soft breath.

"If you could suspend your anger for a few minutes, I will answer all your questions and make an offer to you that will change your life in magnificent ways."

"I've seen how you change lives. I am curious to know how you will explain away the trail of dead people that led me here."

"Well, then, I will have to settle for curiosity."

He looked directly into my eyes as he spoke. He didn't blink. He was "in full agreement with everything he said," an expression Carl had often used to describe the sociopath who sings to one choir: himself. Cromwell continued.

"You should know first what prompted the building of NEAR Earth. I used to like people. Then I realized that we, all of us, only actually like very few people. The more of us there are, the more we rub against each other, like rats in a science experiment."

He looked to me as if for affirmation and went on with his macabre "sermon."

"When the cage gets too crowded, even if there is enough food, the rats turn on each other. It isn't survival, it is selection. It is nature, and life in the raw is seldom mild. The world is rubbed raw, Detective Edo. It goes beyond the people themselves."

I had no response.

"Human beings," he explained, "eventually destroy everything they build, unless they think they have already destroyed it. Then they abandon it. I love the paradox of our landfill: built of destruction. No one would think to look here for perfection: the perfect place for the perfect place. It is where I want to start over, with just a few people, but with all the good resources and technology and knowledge that will move us forward in a new way."

He wanted some reply, or a sign of agreement, or argument, so he waited. My turn.

"Why do it this way? Just in order to accomplish this, you have murdered, manipulated, and extorted your way to perfection. If the world is that terrible, why not have this place as a haven, open to the ones you want, a shining example instead of a secret?"

He smiled knowingly, "Because there have always been such havens for higher ideals and guess what happened to them? The Library of Alexandria, the treasure house of the ancient world's knowledge, was largely burned to the ground by a careless Julius Caesar. Over time, political and religious mobs destroyed what was left, knowing what they destroyed and enjoying the destruction. The United Nations crouches like a toothless lion in the face of real conflict. I won't bore you with the list of failures."

"But we keep making the attempt. Why not be part of that?" I wanted to know.

"I have the solution, and I don't wish to wait. I have planned for ten years, selected 100,000 people with all the physical, mental, and spiritual skills and talents we will need. With everything nearly in place, I need to put my plan into action now. We have the ability to clear the Earth of the unwanted, without destroying the infrastructure, which is useful, or the environment, which is essential. In fact, we will be improving the environment by halting all the many human endeavors that have polluted it. The Earth will begin to recover immediately."

Terror struck deep as I realized Cromwell was no longer planning, he was enacting, and had already twisted brilliant technology into a bio-weapon. I forced the fear out of my voice and said, "The sickness: I've seen it work."

He looked at me in astonishment. Sudden emotion did not sit well on his face. He thought for a moment, then his eyes widened.

"You sent that man. He was always at the sales, but he went too far this last time. That is a point in your favor, Detective, an interesting approach. So you know what I have in mind, just on a much, much larger scale. We have landfills worldwide, near every major population area, and countless smaller facilities. They all have our trademark blue and white collection vehicles, everyone is used to seeing them," he revealed.

I could see he was proud of his plan.

"They pass near almost every building on every street, all over the world, collecting the garbage and recyclables," he said. "Except that, one day soon, they won't be only collecting, they will be dispersing. In unison around the globe, they will be sending our contagion into the air, along with their exhaust. We have misting equipment installed on rooftops as well, to cover every area. All the landfills will be giving off the same contamination, described as a sanitizer. It will be so true!"

Cromwell eyed me triumphantly.

"By the time anyone can suspect, it will be too late. Everyone will be so ill so quickly that there will be few able-bodied people to search for the source of the illness. Even remote areas will be affected. The air belongs to us all, for good or ill. It will be over rapidly, if not painlessly. Then the healing of the Earth can begin. Any small pockets of survivors will hail our appearance with thanksgiving."

"With billions of dead bodies lying around, the Earth might take longer to heal than you think," I speculated.

He actually laughed.

"The bodies will be no difficulty. Human remains are so corruptible, so readily decomposed and consumed. My scientists tell me it could take about eighteen months for the animals and the atmosphere to do their work."

"And these scientists, your scientists that you no doubt bought, have told you they know exactly how this contagion will behave, that it will die with its host, and not dream of mutating into something else in order to survive. That is what all living things try to do, you know, survive," I said. "Can they be sure this little germ doesn't want the Earth for itself?"

Cromwell's eyes shifted slightly away from me. I knew that sign and acted on it. "You're not really sure, are you? Buying the science doesn't guarantee the result, does it?"

"You of all people should not be surprised by how money changes a person's allegiance to his own ideals. Still, you are very insightful, Detective Edo. You have hit on the reason I need you most. Time will erode patience while we wait for the Earth to clean itself."

"You want an enforcer, in case this Earth turns out to be the only Earth available after all. Perfection may carry a heavy price."

"Overstated, as I'm sure all will be well, but, you understand. Excellent, Detective."

"Someone showed me recently the problem with perfection. It is usually only perfect from one person's viewpoint, so that person has to convince others that what they are seeing is perfection. That is why we are here, so you can convince me that this is a great and wonderful thing. Let me tell you about enclosed places."

I didn't wait for his reaction, but went on. "I used to decompress in a LastSteel dome when I was a deep diver. I could be there hours, waiting for the nitrogen to leach back out of my blood. I had claustrophobia, but I knew that going in, and I wanted to conquer it. I wrote in a journal to do something else with my mind for those hours rather than think about that eight-foot space I occupied with two other people. They were ex-police divers, and they didn't suffer from claustrophobia. They were really happy with the pay, and very relaxed for the first two months of dives."

I had leaned toward Cromwell. He mirrored me, drawn into my account. I continued.

"Then something strange happened. Since they had never needed to fend off that fear I had, they had no tools to fend it off as it began to grow. They tired of their vieunits and circular conversations. They stopped giving me a hard time about my writing and started their own journals. They had a ritual before each dive, lining up their pens and notebooks just so, for their stay in the dome." Cromwell was intently listening.

"One night, after five months, they found both notebooks, but only one pen. One attacked the other over the single pen before I could even offer mine. They finished decompression and left the oil rig that night. Neither ever returned."

I knew I had drawn him in, and he was hooked. I continued, "Your problem here will not be something huge, at first. You have all this space, or so it seems now. After a while, it will lose its charm, as all artificial things do, and ritual will set in to counteract the confinement. Some people will want the sky to be just the way it was the night before, or each chair placed just so, because if it isn't, they will run screaming down the paths or kill the person who moved the chair. If you are lucky, they'll be horrified, wondering why they have lost their minds over a chair or over a sky. If you are not lucky, they will put the chair back in its place and feel safe again, until the next time. Trouble in paradise, Cromwell."

I suddenly remembered why I recognized his name.

"A girl named something like Allison, Alicia … Cromwell, collided with a bridge. She had to be related to you."

His face broke.

"Allison, My daughter. She knew everything. She was to be the jewel in the crown. Then she met one of the workers here, someone who was not intended to experience the future, if you understand me."

"Oh, an imperfect one. She loved an imperfect one."

"If you had children, Detective, you might understand my pain. She simply wouldn't see that he was wrong for her. We struggled over it for months. I tried to pay him off, but there didn't seem to be a price that interested him. She wouldn't hear of his being sent away either."

"They actually loved each other. How inconvenient."

I could have said anything, because he was not hearing me now. He was still trying to convince his lost daughter of his good intent.

"Allison wanted to go away with him, even if it meant they would miss the window of opportunity to be included in NEAR Earth. Why couldn't she see that? Then, a miracle occurred, and he was killed. He was stabbed by a coworker while trying to stop a fight."

He practically rubbed his hands together. "It was such a random thing. I had nothing to do with it. Even Allison knew it was chance—or fate. She grieved, and clung to me, and went on with her life. The night she was to appear at her debut, she took extra care with her appearance. She had selected a gown I admired; she wore her hair just as I liked it. She wanted to make a grand entrance, so she took her own craft. Just minutes from where we were waiting, she overrode the autopilot with a handheld device, which she threw out her window just as she flew into the commuter bridge."

He paused, "The police did not find it, my staff found it. She left no note. The device was the only thing that revealed her plan. People in the train just past the impact point said the craft almost hit them but swerved left and they were unharmed. She spared them, my Allison spared them. She did not spare me."

His face was covered with the past. Sometimes in an interview, when a suspect has reached that lowest ebb, the truth is there at the bottom, and it is a relief to find it.

"What happened to Claire Levitt?"

"She was so lovely. When they brought me her file, she struck a chord with me. She looked a bit like Allison. I knew I had to have her, that she could perhaps revive the dream. We picked her up much the same way we found Jack. She was exhilarated by the idea of founding a new world. Claire adored this place. She liked the very chair you chose."

"So what happened?"

"Unfortunately, she began to manifest exactly the behavior you described. She cut off her own finger, saying it had carried a ring from the old life like a noose she had to escape, yet she wanted her parents. We would find her curled up under a tree, or walking at night in the dark, and she would run from us like a wild animal."

I remembered Jana's remark about the plant matter on her feet.

"Claire had grass stains on her feet, but no sign of any dirt. How is that possible?"

"Detective, just below the grass is a grid mounted over a hydroponics layer that feeds the trees and greenery. You see, I really don't like dirt. We have the cleanest environment on Earth here. Even the lake bed isn't sand but a fabric to imitate sand, with gel under it that accepts the imprint of your feet in a remarkable imitation of walking in a lake bed."

I focused on the horrible use rather than the ingenuity.

Cromwell continued, "As I was saying, Claire became unmanageable. We were afraid she would find a way out, to go to her parents and tell them about this place and try to bring them. We couldn't have that. While determining what to do with her, I had a revelation. Her condition made me realize we would need to control certain people, and also control the controllers. We couldn't just have executioners; we had to have someone in charge."

He looked directly at me, "I went through our files, and there you were. You had the credentials, and we had your brother. However, I knew you wouldn't come to us the way Jack did. Jack is weak. I often think of him as the son I never had—the disappointing son I never had. No, you would need persuasion of a different kind. You had to be intrigued. You had to have answers. So you have your answers. What do you think?"

I didn't respond.

"You really only have two choices. You can see the opportunity here. Can't you feel the green quiet of the future I am offering you, where you could travel a thousand miles and not encounter another soul, compared to this world with other humans not farther than a few feet away no matter where you are? Besides, the only other option is death, and not just your own. If what you said is true, that all living things try to survive, your choice should be obvious."

I countered, "Yet both your Miss America and her runner-up said no to your opportunity. Maybe they thought survival wasn't living. Maybe I don't either."

He had changed. His face was harder, as if it had cooled in a mold. Cold anger is hard to counter. I would try.

"So now what will you do? No queen for your kingdom."

He smiled, which was more chilling than the mask.

"There is another …"

He stood suddenly and brushed off the top of his sleeves, when they had touched nothing. It was a gesture of preening, or shedding, like a snake discarding a skin.

"You are right, Detective Edo, about perfection. I was willing to include you in our endeavor, when you have been so imperfect. From the moment you knew the truth about the girl, about Claire, you began to make mistakes. You sent your partner away to protect her, a clear indication she meant something to you, which is the best way to make her a form of leverage, if that is what we had wanted. You went to your parents. We saw you. You avoided being followed, but it didn't matter. We were already waiting there! I have to say your parents have been clever so far."

My parents. My face must have given away my sudden alarm.

"Oh, we haven't found them yet, but we will, or, it will be too late to matter. You met your forensic specialist at the Annex and then sent her away and altered her reports, which is a complete breach of conduct. By the way, Jana thanks you for the free vacation."

"Jana?" I said out loud. "She's involved?"

"Yes, Detective, it was another proof that all your skills were compromised by your being too close to the case. Jana played you like a fish on a line. You have made every possible error in judgment, yet that is why I wanted you. You were loyal and would put your job and life at stake for your family. This could have been your family. We could have been your family. Instead, you have made the ultimate error in judgment. You are not just imperfect. You are stupid, and now you will be dead."

His speech had hit home. *Jana. God! How could I have been so blind?* She was the agent, so helpful, so frightened, and so good at her job. He was right, about everything. I put my head down, for a moment. Yet, he had given me one hope. My parents were still free. I was still their son, and I had perhaps saved them, if only for now.

I stood up and realized I felt nothing he wanted me to feel. I took a step toward him, and he moved to the side. There was no fear on either part. He had someone nearby who would kill me wordlessly at his signal. My lack of fear had no such support. It stemmed simply from knowing I had done what I could for those I loved from day to day, and there was no fear or shame in that. I walked past him and he turned to see what I was doing. I smiled and spoke as I set to work.

"Here, let me put your chair back in its place. The ritual might as well start now."

I lifted the chair and set it down in the row. I gave it a slight adjustment by pulling on one wide armrest, which allowed me to pull the transmit comunit from the underside with my fingertips and smoothly palm it. I reached up to pull at the necktite as if it were hurting me and transferred the comunit to the inside fabric of my shirt collar as I did. It was one of the pair I drew from my slacks pocket and attached to my shirt hem when I got up from the floor of the Masher. I had planted the other one on Jack when I fell against him. I only hoped he'd heard it all.

Cromwell had already turned and continued toward the unseen vehicle. His voice curled back over his shoulder like smoke rising in the air.

"You'll be taken to your brother. He has plans for you."

19

Two huge guards materialized and walked me to the entrance Jack had escorted me through, where he was waiting in the hallway. I turned to take a last look at... what? The future, connected to the worst version yet of a recurring nightmare from our human past, a holocaust. I was certain Cromwell fully intended to do exactly what he had said, and soon.

Jack took me at gunpoint without a word, but the necktite constricted enough to force me to breathe with my mouth open, like a child with a cold.

With the guards trailing us, we retraced our path to the receiving dock. They holstered their weapons and left us. Jack and I donned the suits and returned to the Masher, the necktite a constant reminder that he walked behind me.

Once we were inside, the suits came off. Jack pointed with his magnum to a railing along the far side of the control room where a set of quick-cuffs hung waiting on a tether. I stopped near them and turned to face Jack.

The necktite constricted until the white haze of unconsciousness floated at the edge of my vision. I fell to my knees. Jack came up suddenly next to me and roughly searched me until he found the comunit. He swung around me expertly to cuff me to the railing, the tether stretching just enough so I could move a few feet either way.

He set his gun on the control console ten feet from us and disappeared, taking a few minutes to return. It may not have been minutes, but seemed that way in my personal world of slow strangulation. Then, the necktite released slowly.

I took deep breaths as Jack spoke from a few feet beyond my radius of movement.

"I couldn't risk your saying anything and having the comunit you planted on me repeat it for his bodyguards."

As I struggled to my feet, I tried to clear my throat, which hurt like hell. My voice was a hoarse whisper. It echoed off the wall behind me.

"Then you heard him, you heard his plan for this place. I think no one knows, and he guessed if I told you, you wouldn't believe me. But I know you believe him. Whatever you are now, Jack, you aren't this. You can't be a believer in this. He's talking about the end of the world, and he can make it happen. It can't happen. You can't be part of this."

"Just shut up for a minute."

I moved as close to him as I could without strangling. My voice became the sound of a rasp, drawn softly across wood.

"You can stop him, Jack. He trusts you. Come with me and we can stop him together. Our parents, don't you care about them, or about the billions of people who will die if he goes through with this?"

Jack seemed to be weighing things. Imprinting on a maniac had to be slowing the process. He thought aloud.

"I was the top here, you know? I was the righthand man. Nothing happened that I didn't make happen, until just about three weeks ago, when he asked me to find a way to bring you here. He used to tell me everything, or so I thought. He never told me, or any of us, this plan. I can't believe he didn't trust me after all this time."

He shook his head, stung by this realization. Maybe I could help drive the wedge a little further between Jack and Cromwell.

"Didn't you ever wonder why he had scientists engineer an illness capable of killing in a matter of hours?"

"He said that was to protect the entrances to NEAR Earth when civilization finally set about destroying itself, when the mobs would be desperate to get to a safe place and might even consider a tunnel in a landfill as protection from radiation. Just this week, the air in all the tunnels was seeded with the bacteria, or whatever it is, in this part of the fill. We have the vaccine. I don't believe it will mutate. You just said that to him to get more information."

"I didn't say it would mutate, he acknowledged it might." I suddenly focused on Jack's last comments. "Wait, you said 'just this week' you seeded the tunnels in this part of the fill."

I closed my eyes and spread the timeline of events out the way Suli and I always did, except I didn't have a screen, or Suli's insight, so I would have to lay it out in my mind.

"And three weeks ago, he asked you to find a way to bring me here. I think I know why he isn't telling you everything any more, and why he had his guards escort us all the way to the exit."

"I don't care what you think you know."

He was lying.

"And Claire had become a problem that had to be solved, maybe about the same time. So you found a way to solve two problems at once. You killed Claire, put her in a vacuum-sealed environment so no one could readily tell her time of death, and moved her to the other part of the fill where she could be found. The tunnel didn't collapse two weeks ago; it was blasted open to make way for the Masher that carried her to the dig site and planted her with the core cutter."

Jack stared at me as I revealed his plan, "Jana, your agent at the precinct, made sure someone called for the detective that was closest to the scene the next day. She made sure it was me. You probably had my squadcraft tagged with a G dot. It's too bad you had to grandstand for your boss. I think he didn't like the attention you got with your problem solving. And you breached the tunnel system. He probably wasn't ready for that, but the damage was done. So he seeded the tunnels after the repair, so there was no chance of that happening again, and hoped that it wouldn't go any farther than that. Then I came to the fill and talked to Reeves, and he knew I was getting too close too soon. You forced him to move up his timeline. I would guess Cromwell doesn't like to be forced."

"Don't use his name."

"Why, is he listening? Are you sure he is, or isn't? Are you sure of anything anymore, Jack?"

"I have magnetic blocking on the skin of the Masher. No one can pick up what we're saying inside, I checked. Just don't say his name. You're not worthy."

I felt the color drain from my face. *Had I lost him? Was blood not enough, was logic not enough? Could the right words change him?* I prayed for the right words. I fought for the right words.

"Jack, I know somewhere in you is the smiling brother who grew up with me in a family, and … do you really think the whole world deserves this fate?"

"Don't you? Every day in your line of work, you see what society has become. You must look at most people with disgust. They pollute everything they touch, they beat their children, and they drink themselves to death, or starve to death. They kill each other in fits of rage. They hate for no reason. They have earned death, all of them."

He spewed this out as a litany: A new version of the Lord's Prayer. How do you start a world with that?

"Your doctrine, or his, Jack?"

"Does it matter? It's true. When someone buys a new home, they empty it of its contents and start fresh. That is the reason for NEAR Earth—to prepare the new home."

"And the new owners, don't they bring any of their faults with them from their old home?"

"That's why he's so careful about those he chooses. You could have been one of the chosen, and if you knew what I know, you wouldn't have refused this chance. I just now understand what he had in mind. He wanted you to come of your own accord, though."

"No one could make me accept."

"What about *someone*?"

20

A single word can stop your heart. Jack smiled a little, and waited for my reaction. I had to ask, he knew I had to ask.

"You found our parents."

He laughed.

"No. He told you we didn't have them. Didn't you wonder what he meant when he said there is another?"

I knew the one Cromwell had already used to bring me this far.

"Jana."

Jack let out a long laugh this time.

"Jana? That righteous, unbending chick-on-a-stick? He would choose her last in a world of billions. Try again."

I searched my memory for any other connection. Then Cromwell's face swam into view. In the Laasn, with Lisbeth, probably hoping I would fall into her offer and into his hands that night, after the cognac.

"Lisbeth Harmon. Cromwell used her to try to get to me."

"Damaged goods, she goes cheap. He likes them clean. Suli is here, sedated, right here in the Masher."

No. No. The dying feeling was back, but had nothing to do with my own death. Jack saw it. He gave me a brittle smile that fell apart after a second.

"Well, Kirt, do you want to change your mind about staying? She is fine. I was waiting for her in her apartment; her door had such an old, easy lock to pick.

"She put up a spirited but short fight before the drug kicked in. I carried her up the fire escape to the roof. Good thing she's light, it was six flights. I even brought her here in her own craft. That way, I can pull it into the fill and make it disappear. She won't even have been missed yet."

Some horrors are larger than the mind can grasp, so it resorts to the simplest thoughts while it copes. Not Suli. Not here. No one would wither and die faster in captivity. This couldn't be happening. The words came forth without effort or hesitation.

"I don't care what you do to me now. Let her go. She will not survive this, any more than she will survive your massacre, but at least she will *not be here.*"

The last words were as close to a shout as my ruined throat could raise. I couldn't stop. "You bastard, you nest of sick bastards who think you know what life is. Life is Suli, and people like her, who see the world and still want it, want to live in it, maybe improve it just by being. They love and they hurt and they die, but they want it anyway. Your fucking, shining, fabricated 'future' can't hold a candle to one minute of her real life. I love her. She has become everything to me. She won't stand for this, I know her. Let her go!"

Jack looked unmoved.

"And what leverage do you have? What have you got to bargain with, Kirt? Cromwell doesn't want you anymore. He does want Suli, I see it now. You were never the main prize, she was."

I had no leverage, he was right. I had only words.

"I was wrong to think there was anything left of you, any part that was good. I hope you and Cromwell rot in here, then rot in hell, but then, I think you are already there."

Without warning, he grabbed my shirt and slammed me sideways down the wall. My hands were still quick-cuffed behind my back. The three-foot tether stretched like a leash from the cuffs to the handrail. Jack hit me across the face with the back of his hand so hard that I reeled. He caught me with one hand around my arm and punched me in the stomach with the other.

I tasted blood. I doubled up and drew back, but came forward with the weapons I had, my head and my legs. I rammed him. He was ready and fended me off with his hands and arms, then tried to hit me in the face again. I turned my head while jerking my knee up into his groin. It worked. He hit the floor beyond my three-foot radius, writhing. He shouted through his pain.

"You fight like a fucking girl!"

"Said the one without the cuffs!"

We both gasped for breath. I spit blood until I cleared my mouth of it. Jack still lay on the floor, breathing sharply, looking at nothing. We didn't speak or move for what seemed like a very long time. I broke the silence.

"Let Suli go. You put her under before you brought her here, so she couldn't lead anyone to you, or find her way out either. I think that's what you did with all of them. She won't even know why she was taken, or what this was about, if you take her back out now."

He finally looked at me. He sat up, but did not get up from the floor, as if he preferred to sit there, looking up at me and said, "With all the women I've had, I never felt for one of them, or had one of them feel for me, what you have with her. You even got that, and I didn't."

Jack still didn't move. He seemed to have grown smaller there on the floor, shriveled by the truth perhaps. He flexed his hands and looked at them as he spoke, "I thought he loved me."

And there it was. The only real reason we do anything is out of love—found or lost. Jack got up slowly, and turned to address me as if he'd just remembered I was there.

"Suli is a very lucky person. She can go back, and not know anything, but neither of us can."

In a sentence, he had told me Suli's fate, and mine.

He walked to the Masher control console and picked up his lasermagnum. He used his remote to release the tether. He deactivated my necktite. I felt it cool my neck—pleasure after pain, a strange afterthought by the inventors.

He pointed the gun at me and gestured with it toward the airlock. I walked ahead of him, hoping for an opportunity to act. He waited until I was standing by the gear, clicked the remote again and the quick-cuffs released.

"Get into that suit, yes, my breathersuit. I'll just borrow this other one. We are going to take a little walk. I think Jack Edo is about to have an accident."

He kept his weapon trained on me as I donned his suit, then closed me in the airlock until he was suited up with the gun ready in his glove. Jack knew I wouldn't open the airlock to the outside. He had the trump card. He had Suli. He opened the airlock and stepped in, then closed the inside door. From the control panel on the wall, he opened the port into inner space.

Time is a bellows, swelling or collapsing to match the events of the moment. Just then, time compressed for me into a rapid nightmare of darkness. I led as we moved away from the Masher toward a faint light about a quarter mile in the distance. My mind was racing. Jack had the gun, what did I have? What weapon did I need?

The whole landfill, the trash, the air itself could be weapons. I stubbed my boot into the path and a twisted piece of metal stuck in the toe of the sole. It was perfect. I knew Jack trailed me by a few steps, close enough to control me but too far for contact. I chose a clear area and stumbled, coming down on one knee. I pulled the metal strip from the boot toe into the maw of my left glove. Jack's voice clicked into my headset.

"Whatever you picked up, drop it. We're almost there. You might as well face me."

I turned to him standing five feet from me, the Masher shining faintly in the distance behind him. His helmet lights showed his face as if he were a disembodied head in the darkness. My helmet lights were off but I voiced them on. We didn't move.

"What are you waiting for, Jack? You have the gun and Suli, and I have a piece of metal that might almost reach you before you kill me, but I would still like to try to kill you. Let's finish it."

He raised the lasermagnum, and I lunged toward him. The beam blinded us both for a moment as it cut into my suit, but I felt nothing. He had missed. I was nearly on him, the metal shard shining in my glove. He sidestepped, faster than I thought he could. I twisted back, but Jack had stepped behind a circle of metal, a gigantic saw blade, partly submerged in the trash. Its ragged teeth curved up and caught hints of light.

"Slow down, Kirt. I wasn't trying to shoot you. Allow me to be generous. There is a way out of this. You're wearing my suit, with both the comunits you planted, intact, including everything Cromwell said, everything we have said."

I couldn't believe what I was hearing.

"Yes, I let you think I took the comunit off your shirt collar, but I left it there, still transmitting. Don't you wonder why? You can get back to the Masher and drive that little girl out of here and into the wild blue and the happily ever after, or the brief ever after. There's only one catch."

He sounded like the old Jack, about to sell me something.

He said, "The suit is compromised, which means you have so little time. Do you want to waste it fighting me? If you actually are as smart as you think, you might live. Each second is your enemy."

He pushed his helmet back and took a deep breath. He suddenly even looked like the Jack I remembered, surprised, and faintly pleased. I was shocked, by everything. I reacted automatically.

"Jack, what are you doing? The atmosphere is lethal."

"Lethal? The atmosphere doesn't worry me. There are other worries, but, in fact, I've never felt better."

"I ... Jack, you could have come with me, I could have helped you."

He spoke over his shoulder as he walked into the darkness. His words were faintly impaired either by some last emotion, or it could have been the fill, starting to have its way with him.

He said only, "Get out of here."

I tried.

21

I was wheezing by the time I reached the Masher. I hit the airlock button while coughing. I got inside and looked at the damage to the suit.

It was really just a hole like any laser burn, but the beam itself had grazed my thigh and passed through a slightly larger hole at the back of the suit leg. It was such a small burn, I hadn't even felt it, but there was already swelling and a yellow discoloration at the wound site.

I have been afraid in my life, but always I could see the source of the fear and take some action. This was different. An invisible army marched through my skin already, laying waste and moving fast.

I stripped off the suit but did not look again at the wound. I was terrified, sweating, and probably already dying, but I had to find Suli and get her out of this hell hole. I willed time to decompress just enough to do that one thing.

I had to wait for the ultraviolet air wash to sterilize the suit, me, and everything in the airlock before the inside port would open. I was out of there just as the fans stopped fully.

The Masher had as many rooms as I had fears. I slammed from one to another, weaving a little now. There she was, on a bunk in the third compartment I checked. She was the only beautiful thing in the whole damaged world and looked more so sleeping. I didn't even take time to move her, but headed to the console.

I vomited on the way there, and sweat was beading at every pore. I fired up the control panel, found the right lighted button, and let the Masher tread its own way on autoguide to the east exit. There seemed to be only one speed: Too slow.

Fuck, damn, I had to put the suit back on, or they would know I wasn't Jack. With his suit, my build, my walk, everything would be enough like Jack to fool the casual observer, I hoped.

I donned the suit and locked down the helmet. I noticed a change in the darkness at the portholes, so we were coming out of the fill through the ultraviolight barrier. The predawn light was both a gift and a threat when the Masher emerged from the fill, because there was a tarmac, with a few workers, but Suli's craft was there, as Jack had said. We ground to a halt automatically. The autoguide ended at the lot.

I went into the compartment to get Suli. She was unresponsive, lost in a heavily drugged sleep. She did moan when I lifted her, but I also moaned. It was like picking up the Earth, I was so weak. I lurched to the exit door, but had to lean against the wall and shift Suli to my shoulder to press the release button.

The dropwalk appeared to sway in front of me. Only eight steps. Seven. Six. I stumbled off the last one and went down on one knee, but Suli was over my shoulder in a fireman's carry. She swayed against my back unharmed.

I struggled up and tried for a nonchalant stroll, but I could not walk naturally, no matter what I willed. I hunched over beneath Suli, my newest hope to just reach her hovercraft.

It was a wasteland of thirty feet. I got to the door of the craft. I had to rouse Suli; her doors were voice-activated if there was no key card. I had no key. I bowed just a little further to rest her against the side of the craft. I tilted back my helmet. If anyone was watching closely, we were finished, but there was no other choice.

I spoke her name hoarsely, but she didn't respond. I spoke her name again. There must have been something in my voice that reached into her dream state. Her head rolled slightly toward me. She opened her eyes, but they wouldn't focus, so she closed them again.

I told her to say "open," and she said the word like a child who has been told to recite before the class.

The door swung upward. People were coming. I rolled her over to the opening and shoved her unceremoniously across to the passenger side. She did not move. I got into the control seat and closed the door.

Two curious workers approached the back of the craft. I hit lift and headed straight up, into, and through the gulls, through the traffic patterns, into clear space, mainly because I was losing consciousness.

Suli stirred as I hit level and the craft held still. In a last moment, I pulled Suli's hair. She yelped, but I whispered directions. I could not be sure she heard me. I didn't even hear my own last words.

22

There was a bird on the window ledge. It fluttered against the light and chance or fate put it between the sun and me. It became a silhouette backed by radiance. *Had I died?* There were ceiling tiles. That seemed too regular for death. I felt fabric under my fingertips and heard the bird trill from the light. Ten seconds of knowledge were too exhausting.

■ ■ ■

Things had changed when I opened my eyes the second time. No fabric under my fingers. Instead, other fingers intertwined with mine. Again, chance or fate put the light behind what had awakened me. A haloed face leaned close and kissed my cheek.

Suli. I felt her more than saw her. My words were a croak.

"How long?"

"Three weeks, two days, and four close calls. Dr. Augustini feels that the injection he ordered for you, when you brought Sniff here, helped, but there was only any real hope because we got you here so quickly. We feared you left us for good. Well, not we. I knew you would have to know the outcome. I knew you had to come back … for us."

I heard and felt the catch in her voice. Her hand traced the side of my face. She laid her head on my chest for a moment, then stood and turned to sit on the edge of the bed facing me. A disturbance in the hall drew itself up like a wave and washed into my room.

Dr. Augustini led a group of interns to my bedside. They pooled around the bed three-deep, some jockeying for position in the back, but most stood as close as they could to him.

"Good morning, at last, Detective Edo. My students and I have been hoping for this day. You have, however, been a source of such learning!"

The group laughed, and huddled closer to their mentor. Dr. Augustini took my hand to shake it, and then smoothly checked my pulse. He turned to Suli.

"Ms. Masters, have you told him?"

"Nothing yet. I wanted to see if he was in working order first." Suli colored slightly. "I mean, I didn't want to exhaust him on his first day back in the land of the living."

Dr. Augustini smiled. I cleared my throat. The interns looked shocked for a moment. I had been a body so long, but never a voice.

"Tell me what?"

I'd spoken three words, but it was, at least, almost a sentence. Suli took my hands. Hers trembled slightly. All fell silent.

"Not just in this room, but in this country and on this continent and in this world, you are a hero. I will bring you the whole official report. You won't believe it, what you did, but for right now, all you need to know is that there has been an international vigil for you. I promise that no one got any images while you have been here, but the media had file footage from your police award ceremonies, and your face is known to everyone on the planet," she said.

I had no words this time.

She continued, "The flowers and cards pile up outside the hospital every day until trucks remove them. The President calls each day about you. When the people of the world learn you are awake, they will stop whatever they are doing and celebrate."

I began to think I had died after all. No one said anything. Suli looked sideways at Dr. Augustini and turned to me again, "They named a country after you."

"A small one," he added.

They looked at each other again and began to laugh. The interns joined them. Suli struggled to get her next words out through bouts of breathless laughter.

"I'm kidding about the country thing. I'm sorry, Kirt, I … just couldn't help myself. It was getting too serious in here, and it has been so serious in here these past weeks, with you nearly dying every other minute."

Suddenly her breathlessness and tears changed and she covered her face. Dr. Augustini turned to his group, raised his hands like an orchestra conductor, and gestured them out of the room. He followed, drawing the door shut between a waiting world and world of just two.

23

I can tell you that sleep is love. After I gathered Suli to me on the bed so she could cry away her relief, we slept for hours. I gained strength and Suli relinquished it, so that we awoke as equals again.

I think Dr. Augustini looked in on us once, but showed his skill as a healer by keeping everyone at bay and by doing nothing, which occasionally is the wiser brother to doing something.

He did finally return at dusk. He knocked politely first, but we had been awake for some time, and Suli sat quietly at the end of my bed as Dr. Augustini checked me over carefully. He looked at Suli.

"My dear, restorative sleep is the finest prescription never written. You are good for him. Now, however, you need to go home and prepare yourself for the onslaught of attention which is coming this way. We will not be able to hold off the world's interest much longer."

"May I bring the report on the NEAR so that Kirt can be fully aware of all that has happened?"

"Tomorrow, yes, by all means. Now, I need to speak with Detective Edo for a moment."

Suli swooped in and kissed me before slipping out the door without another word. Dr. Augustini turned to me and spoke in the gentlest of voices.

"There are always consequences when we take things into our own hands and out of God's hands. You are recovering well, but you may have some lingering effects of this illness. Because it was engineered, the contagion may have some last revenge, even if its intended victim should somehow survive. Given that it was supposed to free the Earth of every last unwanted human being, what do you think that revenge might be?"

Before I could speak, he put up his hands, palms together for a moment, in a gesture of supplication. "Detective Edo, I should never have put it as a question to you. I am sorry, how stupid of me! Let me get to the point of the matter. You must stay in touch with me. Contact me if anything seems unusual about your health. Let us remain vigilant. If some scientist can engineer epigenetic markers, I can engineer a reversal."

On that strange yet hopeful note, he ordered me to rest. I remained attached to machines and IV feeders while I slept. They watched over me, humming electric lullabies.

The morning brought Suli and the report vieunit as promised. Brian Shand came beaming into the room with her, but stood back for a moment.

"Is it okay to approach the deity?" He then bounded forward, almost knocking over the IV drip, and shook my hand.

"You look terrible, but a lot better than I expected. We brought you a little hologram report, about three hours of it. It has everything, all the transcripts from the comunits, all the SWAT reports from the sites around the world, live action, just about the most amazing thing anyone has ever seen or read,"

His enthusiasm was matched only by his pride in his role, "Actually, I wrote a lot of the final summary, so I guess I shouldn't say things like 'most amazing,' but really, it is. I'm talking a lot because I'm not sure what to say, except, wow, you did a great thing. That thing you said about life, and the world? Well, my girlfriend, the one I called, the one we met at the landfill? She cried for half an hour when she heard that. We watched the whole thing together. Her name is Lassia, isn't that an incredible name?"

He seemed to have stopped, although I couldn't be certain. The three of us spent an hour just being friends, catching up on my lost three weeks, talking about anything. Suli told me Mrs. Albury sent her best wishes, and that she, and Clyde, missed me.

Suli went on, laughing, telling us how Mrs. Albury, upon learning I was recovering, had bought several pairs of men's shoes for Clyde to chew on until my return. I felt that I was "back," back to the normal world.

Brian had left, but Suli dimmed the room lights just before leaving, sensing I might need to process the story on my own. I projected the report with the vieunit. It was difficult to watch. It threatened that normalcy I had just recovered. We had come so close to losing it all.

My last words to Suli when she was coming out of her drugged state started the report. They were almost unintelligible, and so much hinged on them.

"Check comunits in this suit for background. Landfill. Brian, everyone, ASAP. RimCity Memorial, Dr. Augustini. Me. ASAP." Thank God for Suli.

Thanks to Brian's way with the I-net, the law enforcement agencies of the world attacked the seven main fill sites almost simultaneously while other teams disarmed the remote sanitizing devices. The holographic displays from the SWAT teams' cameras revealed how unprepared the outside workers were for the assault, but also revealed how many of the top scientists and organizers escaped, as well as Jana. That was the handywork of Jack and Cromwell.

The images from the various sites were astounding when projected in my hospital room. Each site was complete and ready for its "select" population. The media made the most of this. The general populations threw themselves against hastily erected barriers, as if destroying the sites would show the intended occupants they were not welcome in the world they would have happily seen die.

Calm was restored in two days, as anger turned to wonder at the technology. Then followed the debate: what was to be done with these places? Some governments argued internally over whether to destroy the sites in their countries. Some were still undecided. Some wanted to keep the atriums as havens for the members of their ruling classes in the event of global war.

I felt cold, cold all over, because I knew Cromwell was safe somewhere, smiling, watching the upper echelon assume control. Perhaps they would succeed where he had not.

Then, something wonderful happened. The government of India decided to offer their site as a home for the destitute families of the workers who had built it. The reason no one had leaked information about the sites was that none of the builders survived the building of them.

The bodies of thousands of captive workers were found crushed together in every fill site, shot dead by their guards when they became too exhausted to be useful. They had been lured away from their desperate circumstances by the promise of jobs at nonexistent companies, and then they simply vanished. They were transported to buildings on the outskirts of the sites and taken through underground tunnels into the work areas. The selected populations would have used the same tunnels to arrive and occupy the sites without attracting attention, but also to reemerge in their new world.

Since the Indian government's decision, some of the families of the Indian workers had already moved into the atrium in Calcutta. Children splashed in the lake while the media stood at the water's edge, sharing the sight with the world.

One boy waded to the shore, still drenched, and he wept, saying through a translator that his father had taught him to swim just before going away forever. The report faded out on his stricken face, his dark eyes overflowing with tears. He and the lake cried together.

The size of the averted disaster made it feel as if the world had peeled out of its orbit, prevented from barreling into the sun only by the nick of a comet that deflected it back on track. I was the comet, a chance comet in the vastest game of chance.

I was no hero. I was a man who had almost failed, but hadn't. And I had good friends, and Suli, and they had also made the difference. In a pool of such thoughts, I tipped my head back into the pillow and closed my eyes, and it all went away. I had at least earned the frailty of sleep.

It was dusk when I surfaced again. Suli was not in the room, but a familiar figure leaned against the window frame, smiling his lazy smile. My former partner.

"Carl, I don't see the pole anywhere."

"Hey, that was only if you came looking for me, I came looking for you. Kirt, you are harder to see than the Pope. In fact, he can't get in to see *you*. I had to use all my clout, or maybe it was the twenty credits."

"Laughing hurts, Carl. Did you bring Linda and Junior?"

"Nope. Hospital rules, FBI, CIA, a few other obstacles."

He came to the bed and put out his hand. I took it and realized how feeble I was. His grip was like a vise.

"So, where does a guy sit in the hospital room of another guy? Apparently, they took out the chairs to allow room for the cast of thousands who treated you. I'll just loom over you."

"Loom away."

"Suli filled me in on her part. Well, that is a partner. That Brian kid did a great job too. While she was bringing you here, Suli gave the heads up to Brian, who got the precinct mobilized. I might be able to forgive him for looking fifteen and making me look sixty. I really didn't think I could see you, but Suli got it to happen. Actually, there isn't anything for me to do, you are in great hands."

He paused. "I came to thank you, wanted to, in person. Because of what you did, Carl Junior will get a chance to grow up, I'll get a chance to grow old, or older, anyway."

We looked steadily at each other for a minute.

"Carl, if you heard or read the full transcripts from the comunits, you know you don't owe only me. It was Jack too. He let me live."

"Wrong. He let you go. You had to do the hard part, the living part, and the saving part, and the almost dying part. He had been vaccinated: he knew he wasn't gambling anything. Jack had the means, method, and opportunity to escape. His is a classic criminal mentality. Kirt, if you could ever do one other thing for me, it would be to accept what he is."

"But he made the decision to put me in his suit. He left the comunits, all the evidence, with me."

"Then he probably destroyed the comunits in the suit he was wearing and pulled out a fresh transmit unit to call and warn Cromwell. It was the only transmission on the unit, something like, 'Go far.' He played both sides, Kirt, but in the end his allegiance was to Cromwell."

"He gave me a chance. He gave the world a chance."

"He called Cromwell, and gave him a chance too. They got away cleanly, without a trace, clever bastards. I can only imagine their next moves. They, together or apart, are two of the sickest pricks on the planet. Maybe we'll get lucky and they'll kill each other."

I was silent. I couldn't blame Carl for his take on things. I had thought the same, until Jack tipped back that helmet.

Even without a chair, Carl managed to be at ease and put me at ease for another hour. I asked if he or Suli or Brian had had any word from my parents, but no. They would know, if they were anywhere within range of any news media, that Jack was alive, but he was not the son they had known. I wondered how or if they would reach me.

24

Suli appeared early the next morning. She had looked so radiant on the previous few days. The change in her was jarring. She carried a small box in her hand. It was unwrapped.

"We had to open it, Kirt. They wouldn't let me bring it in until it was examined and checked out in every possible way, not that it helped. We don't know what it means, but I have a terrible feeling you do."

She handed it to me and stood just at my elbow. It was the paperweight, the cobalt blue wave shining innocently in the sun. It had with it a simple note on a white square of paper.

Jack had written, "As I said, you talk in your sleep, even a drugged sleep. Lucky me."

I suddenly knew what three weeks may have cost me. I might be too late, but I had to try to find my parents before Jack could.

I tossed the note down, threw back the sheet, and put my feet on the floor before Suli could even react. She recovered in time to keep me from collapsing. She was strong enough to help me across the room, trailed by the IV drone and other hookups, and wise enough to stay silent as I saw myself in the bathroom mirror for the first time since waking from the coma.

I stared at a stranger. My bearded face could have been the portrait of an ancestor, perhaps Dr. Kirtland. While I turned my face from side to side and reacquainted myself with me, I gave Suli a quick summary.

"The paperweight is a souvenir of a trip I took with my parents to California. Jack didn't join us. He went to Tahoe with friends instead. I was thirteen and didn't have a choice, but the trip was one of the best experiences of my life."

Suli stood next to me, looking at our images in the mirror.

"And…?" she asked.

"We stayed at a resort with a restaurant named the 'Blue Moon,'" I continued.

"We had dinner there so often my mother and the owner, Wanda, became friends."

"What does that have to do with now?" Suli asked.

"Just before you and I ended up in the NEAR, my parents sent a box with an old door key and a piece of blue paper with the number 1345 on it. Long story short, it was a riddle. I obsessed over it until I solved it: the paper had a watermark of the moon, the 1345 was a street address, the next street over from my parent's house, and the key opened the door. My mother left the paperweight as a clue to finding the next clue without saying the name of the place, out of an abundance of caution in case someone else found the house. She also left a note, and there was a Ninex in the garage for my escape. I left everything there, thinking it was safe."

Suli had let me pour out the backstory. She steepled her hands in thought and said, "I think you had 1345

Blue Moon uppermost in your mind because it was so important to you, and you probably said those exact words in your drugged state, possibly more than once. Jack took notice, did the research, found the house."

I knew she was right. I had an idea.

"Please, Suli," I asked, "See if you can find a blue Ninex registered to my father, or mother. Maybe Jack hasn't abandoned it yet."

Suli smiled.

"On it," she said. "Might take some digging. Your parents have been brilliant at covering their tracks. Now please get back in bed."

Once she had me settled to her satisfaction and had plumped my pillows, Suli thought for a moment and said, "You should keep the beard and moustache, or at least a tamed version of them. You need the anonymity your new look affords you."

"Good idea," I said.

"Kirt, your clean-shaven image is all over the I-net and innewsvapor reports and stories worldwide," she continued. "There are also life-sized holograms of you, so you could be identified from any angle. Weeks in a hospital bed have stolen some of your muscle and weight, so the holograms might actually mislead a few people for a short, but vital, interval."

"Let's get Carl and Brian," I said, "and get them up to speed. I've lost three weeks. Every second counts."

Getting out of Rim City Memorial undetected was going to take some planning. The media monitored every entrance, exit, window, and exhaust vent. Carl, Suli, Brian, and I met two hours later. We brainstormed on my escape, sitting in the chairs someone had finally thought to reinstate in my room. It was great to be allowed out of bed and off the med machines. Suli had brought clothes for me. I finally felt like part of the team again, rather than an object of attention.

We decided there was no chance of posing as a doctor or departing on a gurney in a body bag. They would be waiting for something like that. Trying to depart as a six-foot-two woman would attract its own kind of attention. The roof was under surveillance. Brian, ever moving, got up, moved to the window, tapped his fingers on the sill. He suddenly turned to us and smiled.

"First we lock off this floor, and only Dr. Augustini gets in, and select interns, only those we ourselves know. Then, let's have a big press conference to reintroduce you to the world. We'll invite the President and heads of state. Every reporter will be there, every obscure news service will come. You will be there, in a way. We'll do a hologram sequence, and I can morph you into your clean-shaven self. You will talk for a few minutes and answer in advance some questions we will net-pose. By the time they start to ..."

Carl interrupted, "They will still expect the real Kirt Edo. They will still have reporters all over, just in case they've been decoyed."

Brian had a smile ready..

"I know. There will be lots and lots of reporters, lots of unknowns from far-flung affiliates, wearing press passes, including this tall, thin, bearded guy from, say, Colorado. He'll file out with the rest, disappointed that Kirt Edo will be staying in the hospital a few more days.

No one will know this reporter started the day as Kirt Edo, and that he has been morphed from one to the other in plain sight."

We all looked at him, trusted him instantly without knowing the details, and nodded approvingly.

He headed to the door and said, "I'll set it up in person. Can't take any chances that our photalks are being picked up somehow. Hey, Kirt, you're pretty cheerful for a guy who is about to stand up the President."

He was gone, down the hall in seconds. I spoke first.

"I'm twenty-five," I said, "and he makes me feel old."

Carl rolled his eyes.

"Tell me about it."

"Don't misjudge Brian," Suli said softly. We both looked at her. "I know he seems almost ridiculously innocent, but you didn't see him working on the saving of this planet—and you. When I wasn't here, I was at the precinct, watching him roll out the troops, send protection to surround this hospital, shut down electricity to the fills worldwide, all while moving around the Cave, pointing, sending detectives scurrying. He was a general, and no one questioned it, they just acted, including me."

Carl and I glanced at each other, trying to imagine it. Suli looked off toward the hospital room windows. She was holding my hand.

"I was talking to myself at one point during that first scramble to action," she continued, "and I was saying something like *I hope Kirt is safe*. Brian turned to me, and he looked, well, like the events of the day had cut down to a harsh past running through him, hiding below that boyish surface. I will never forget his next words. He stopped what he was doing, stood still, which he never does, and said, 'Suli, no one will reach Kirt. You have my life on that.'"

Carl said nothing at first. I couldn't have spoken anyway.

After a long pause, Carl looked over at me and said, "Now you know how it feels, how I felt after you ..."

His voice softened. "Things have a way of coming around, don't they?"

He'd been sitting across from me but moved to the chair on my right. After mentally upgrading our mutual respect for Brian, we all tried to recenter ourselves in the present. Carl picked up his train of thought on the escape.

He looked frustrated.

"Give me something to do," he growled.

"Carl," I said, "you will go to the Blue Moon in Cal, and tell Wanda the owner that you represent me. I'll give you something to tell her only I would know, my mother's nickname for Wanda, which is Blondie. She can forward a message to my parents that I'm fine, and to ignore anything they hear or see regarding me, my health, or my whereabouts until I can get to Wanda myself."

"I'll bet Jack is watching the place, assuming you'll try to do just that," Carl offered.

"That's why you're perfect for the job, Carl. My parents will know your name. They met you. Jack never did, and you haven't been in the news like Brian and Suli have. You could walk right by Jack and he wouldn't know you have anything to do with me."

Carl gave me a chilling look.

"Can I hit Jack while I walk right by him?" he asked. "I've seen his age-accelerated image enough times to know that face."

A sadness swept over me as I realized how much the world hated my brother, and how much of that hate he deserved.

"Not much chance of that, Carl," I said. "Jack's too good at hiding. Leave him to me. Brian will get you a low-profile commercial flight, directions, all that. Thanks in advance for doing this. It keeps my options open regarding how I will reappear in the world, and when, and to whom."

"You know, Kirt, I wish it was only Jack we had to deal with. What about the weeks after we get you out of here? Someone, somehow, will figure things out, or you'll be identified by some facial recognition device without warning. They'll be on you in seconds, and I don't mean reporters. Hell, we could handle them six at a time. It's the unfriendlies that worry me. We have to assume Cromwell and others are simmering away somewhere, just waiting for a chance at you."

I turned to Suli, "How much do you love this face? We may have to change it a little in a few weeks."

Carl looked at each of us and, sensing he had disappeared from our circle of thought, excused himself.

Suli got up from her chair and turned to kneel in front of me. I couldn't have that. I stood up and pulled her with me. She touched the side of my face gently and stroked my hair a bit, as if memorizing me.

I put my hand over her hand as she said, "I'll know you no matter what."

25

In short, it worked exactly as Brian said it would. I came off the elevator from the floor my room occupied, in a scrubs top, in a swarm of interns surrounding Dr. Augustini. His presence so captivated the media that they focused on his announcement that Detective Edo was on the adjacent elevator. They raced to position themselves at the door ten feet to our right. The interns surrounding me shielded me as I slipped off the green shirt and joined the media melee, wielding a holocam that blocked part of my face.

No one bothered to look at my bland baggy suit, or at my press badge swinging from the lanyard around my neck. Brian had found a pair of glasses for me that distorted my eyes if seen through them, but they also distorted my vision. I shuffled along, which fit my new persona.

We all complained when there was no one on the elevator and proceeded to the press room downstairs, where we were treated to the hologram of me that Brian had created. It did not satisfy.

When it became clear that Kirt Edo was not attending, was "not quite up to it after all," as Dr. Augustini informed us, the President was interviewed instead. I stood on the outskirts of the mob, with the other lesser luminaries who had fewer teeth and claws than those who got closer. The President was gracious, considering his was the fall-back performance at this failed event.

I moved toward the door among a gang of media personalities. Their voices smoked with anger as they cursed Kirt Edo, even though he was supposedly only delaying his unveiling for a few days. I had to hide a smile. Worship could flower and die quickly.

Outside, I searched my unfamiliar pockets and switched to the sunglasses I found. A wallet with fake ID, my Blade, and a keycard were the other discoveries. I scanned the area and spotted the old model GX Flyer with a Colorado Li-D on the side matching the card. It looked as if it belonged to the new me. Brian had left nothing to chance. The act of climbing aboard healed me. I had not been in a world unfiltered by a hospital room for weeks, and I had to steady my hands as I took the controls and lifted into the morning.

Everything was ahead for me, with no guarantees. Everything was ahead for all of us. Unless I had to kill my brother.

ACKNOWLEDGEMENTS

Special Thanks To:

Nika Cassaro, for a splendid cover design; The great team of Lisa, Ellie, and Rachel at Concierge Marketing, for helping me bring my book to the world; Sandra Wendel, for her insight and editing; All my family, for keeping the faith; Hal Miller, for just about everything else.

If you liked *The NEAR*, join Detective Kirt
Edo as he fights on two new fronts, personal
and planetary: is his criminal brother Jack
closing in on their fleeing parents? What
mystery blight withers the American
heartland? Look for *The FAR*, a new
enviro-terror adventure, coming soon.

Turn the page for a taste of *The FAR*

AN EXCERPT FROM
THE FAR

The Blue Moon Restaurant had changed little in the dozen years since I'd last seen it. I could not say the same for the owner/hostess, who looked up from her stand as I approached.

I remembered her as a confident figure. Now, she appeared wary and hesitant.

"It's Wanda, yes?" I asked.

She used the stand as a sentry tower, to observe and defend.

"How do you know my name?" she asked, "Should I know you?" She looked at me intently and changed her question. "Might I know you?"

"I came here with my parents every night for almost two weeks when I was thirteen."

"Your parents," she said slowly.

"Yes, Quintin and Julia Edo. My mother calls you 'Blondie.'"

Even in the low light, I saw her grow pale, then suddenly regain her proud strength. She exhaled and smiled.

"Let me get someone to seat you....Kirt."

"I didn't come for dinner," I replied, "I came to...."

"Oh, you did come for dinner, and you will eat dinner on the terrace," she commanded, fully restored to leadership.

Wanda made a strange gesture in the air, touching each of her fingertips to her thumb and spreading her fingers at the end.

A server with a long white apron appeared and wordlessly led me out toward the sea side of the restaurant. I looked back at Wanda, who had returned to guard duty. The early hour accounted for the scarcity of customers.

I was glad—or was I? The waiter laid a menu on a table for four and pulled out one of the chairs that hugged the terrace railing.

"I usually choose my own seat," I said politely.

"Not today," he replied, and stood behind the chair, waiting, until I sat down as requested. "I'm Kyle."

"Well, Kyle, are you choosing my meal and the wine?"

He might have considered smiling, but some gravity of circumstance kept him from it.

"No, you decide what you would like, but I may have a suggestion or two."

That sounded so normal that I was caught off-guard for a moment, but Kyle leaned down and opened the menu before me to reveal a handwritten note, and I knew normal had died at the Blue Moon door.

Made in the USA
Charleston, SC
29 November 2014